# HEX AFTER FORTY

M.J. CAAN

Copyright © 2020 by M.J. Caan

All rights reserved.

No part of this book may be reproduced in any form or by any electronic or mechanical means, including information storage and retrieval systems, without written permission from the author, except for the use of brief quotations in a book review.

*For Himself. Because you're simply the best.*

# 1

The first thing Torie Spitz intended to do after her divorce, was head to her lawyer's office and have her name changed back to her maiden name of Bliss. She had never admitted it to anyone, but she hated the name Spitz. It made her sound like the butt of a mean girl's joke from her high school days. Of course, at the time, she had been more than happy to take on her husband's name. It was what was expected of her after all.

Okay, so technically it wasn't the first thing she did. The first thing she did was cry. But she was too ashamed to admit that the man she had spent the past twenty-six years of her life with had reduced her to tears on the evening he announced he was leaving.

When he said it, so casually over a glass of cabernet, she was more than a little confused.

"Leaving? I'm sorry, did you have a work trip that I forgot?" she had asked. She started to panic almost immediately, thinking she had forgotten he had to leave for a business trip and she had not packed his things. He often took the overnight flights to Europe for business, so announcing that he was leaving at five o'clock in the evening wasn't all that strange.

"No," he said with a heavy sigh. "I mean...I'm leaving." He let his words hang in the air, long enough for their meaning to drill their way into Torie's head.

She sat back in the plush dining chairs, unable to focus.

He reached for her hand, which she immediately snapped back.

"What I mean is—" he started.

"I know what you mean," she said. Her voice was soft and sounded especially far away, even to her.

He took a deep breath, ran his hand through his pale blond hair. "We should talk about this."

For some reason, his tone infuriated her.

"Now?" she snapped. "You want to talk now, after you've obviously already made up your mind?" She wanted to fight but felt the energy sapped from her body like air escaping a balloon. The atmosphere around her vibrated in her vision, and she felt a migraine forming in the recesses of her mind.

"Look, you knew this was coming. You had to know…"

Her head snapped up, her eyes locking onto him with an icy gaze. "Knew? You want to know what I thought I knew? I thought we had counseling in our future, yes. I thought that now that Shawn was out of the house and away at college, we would focus on us. On rediscovering what we might have lost over the past few years. That's what I thought I knew." Her hand was trembling, and she didn't trust herself to pick up the glass of wine that enticed her from just a few inches away. "Why don't you tell me what *you* knew?"

Ward looked at the woman he had spent all his adult life with. The mother of his child. The woman that had been his rock and guiding north when he was building his company from the small one-bedroom apartment they rented just out of college. That small business was now one of the biggest telecommunication firms on the planet with contracts all over Europe and Central Asia. But she was more than all that. She was—or had been—his best friend.

"Tor—" he started, then saw her flinch at his pet name for her, "Torie…I guess I just haven't been happy for a while now. I've felt it…"

She saw his mouth moving, but his words had trailed off. He guessed? Guessed?

What the hell did he mean he guessed? Theirs was a marriage; not a goddamned jar of marbles sitting in a grocery window that would win you a year's worth of free Gatorade if you guessed the right number. She felt her heart rate begin to pick up, and the back of her neck felt flushed.

"What's her name, Ward?" she blurted out, silencing him mid-ramble.

He stared at her, swallowing loudly. "Nothing will come of that, Torie. There is no need to add injury to insult here."

Idiot. For someone who worked in the media, he never was very good with words. "I think I should get to be the judge of what hurts and what doesn't." She wanted to say that he had just hurt her, but she bit that back.

"Fine. It's Wednesday. And before you say anything, we never meant for this to happen."

Of course. She had thought it was his little secretary that he claimed not to fawn over, but that would have made him a walking stereotype.

*Wednesday.*

His business partner. Honestly, that one hurt Torie more than if it had been his secretary. His partner, who had come in on the ground floor of the company and managed the client side of the business while Ward—while she *and* Ward, had worked to develop the software integrations that allowed developing countries to greatly reduce load times for web and news aggregate sites.

It hurt so much because Wednesday was what Torie had always wanted to be; the successful business woman. Torie wanted to be the person who was equal to her spouse in love and business. Wednesday was the type of woman that Ward had said he didn't want. He had always wanted his wife to stay home and take care of the house. The more successful they were, the more he domesticated Torie. The fact that Wednesday was so power driven and business focused was one reason she had flown in under Torie's radar.

She wasn't a threat in Torie's eyes.

Torie didn't think twice when she would drop into the fifth

avenue office to see her husband unannounced. She would be relieved to see the perky little blonde sitting at her receptionist desk just outside of Ward's office. She would breathe a sigh of relief to hear that Ward was at a luncheon with Wednesday. Better her than the twenty-five-year-old secretary.

When had it happened? Was it all the trips they took? No, they never traveled together. That was what allowed them to grow the business so fast; divide and conquer Wednesday had said. So if not then, when?

"Torie...are you listening?" he was saying, leaning in towards her.

She recoiled, the sight of him was making her sick. "What? No, I'm not listening, Ward. You're leaving me? For your business partner? How long has it been going on?"

He hesitated. "Six months."

What? Was that even possible?

"Wait," said Torie, "please tell me she isn't pregnant."

"No. Of course not. I guess...I mean, I know it sounds quick. But it's been building for some time now. It was the night we celebrated the acquisition of that start-up from Belgium. We were celebrating and—"

She waved him off. "No, Ward; spare me the gory details. So what are we going to tell Shawn?"

"He's old enough now to understand things like this. I was thinking we could tell him together when he comes home for summer."

Torie's mind was whirling at the thought. "No. I...we can't ruin his summer with this. You made the decision to spring this on me without consideration of how I felt. We won't do that to our son."

"So what are you suggesting?"

"I suggest that we wait until the fall. He's got that trip planned with his friends, so let him enjoy that. As far as he's concerned, you're off on a trip all summer. But we don't tell him we are..." she hesitated, unable to force the words from her mouth. "Giving up on our marriage."

Tears, hot and painful, streaked her face suddenly. She threw the glass of wine she was drinking across the room, hearing it ping into a thousand shattered pieces on the marble floor of the dining room. Surprisingly, it made her feel better and allowed her to gain control over her emotions.

Ward looked at her, his eyes wide in wonder.

"And that's why I thought it best that I take my things and move out as soon as I told you." He slid himself back from the table slowly.

"No, you didn't. Don't you look at me like I'm some violent offender you're afraid will do you bodily harm." Even though the thought was tempting to her. "You decided to run out as soon as you told me because you can't wait to run into the arms of your...what do you even call her? Your *girlfriend*?"

He seemed indignant at the implication. "She is my lover if you must know."

Torie scoffed. "Your lover? Christ."

He left her, sitting at the table, staring at a very expensive cut of swordfish. She realized that one of her favorite cuts of fish would forever be tainted now by the memory of what had just happened. She pushed the plate away from her in disgust. One more thing on the long list of things that would make her hate her husband.

She was still sitting there when he returned, a single black Prada duffel bag slung across his shoulder.

"Um, I'll have the lawyer give you a call tomorrow," he said.

She hadn't even thought about that. They had a family lawyer that had set up Shawn's trust and handled all their affairs. But did she need a separate one? Would their joint lawyer handle this type of family affair? And if he did, to whom would he be more loyal? She rattled through her memories of dealings with him, remembering that Ward had thrown a lot of business at their lawyer's firm over the years. Instinct told her she needed her own lawyer, but right now she was simply too drained to know where to even start with that.

She said nothing as he stood there, looking at her.

What did he want? A kiss goodbye? A handshake? She felt her rage boiling up again as she looked at the plate of uneaten food and briefly imagined him wearing it. Ward must have sensed her thoughts, because he turned his back and headed out of the dining room. She heard the tiny beep from the alarm system as he opened the garage door, followed by the vroom from the engine of his ridiculously overpriced sports car.

Once he was gone, she let out a deep breath; one that felt like she had been holding in for an hour. Then she leaned forward, rested her face in her hands, and cried.

She let herself grieve for almost an hour as she sat there before dragging herself up to the master suite. She looked around and decided there was no way she could sleep in that bed. If she were going to toss and turn all night, it might as well be in a bed that she hadn't shared with *him*.

She wandered into one of the guest suites and looked around. There were seven bedrooms in the house, and she realized she had never actually slept in any of them. She plopped down on the mattress, relieved to find it was surprisingly comfortable, and decided that it would do for now. Tomorrow, the first thing she planned to do was have the master bed removed from the house and burned. No, that was second. First would be a call to her best friend, Freya, and then the lawyer; and then the bed.

Satisfied with a game plan, she went into the guest bath, filled the soaking tub with warm water, tossed in a bath bomb that exploded in an array of colors, and lazed there until she felt herself sufficiently drowsy to sleep.

She was right; the bed was comfortable, and the thousand-count Egyptian-cotton sheets lulled her off to dreamland almost immediately.

She awoke to the annoying buzz of her cell phone. She ignored it, turning over and bending the pillow around her head. Then the phone rang again, and she feared it might be Shawn calling. She panicked, thinking Ward had called him anyway to tell him God knows what. Bolting upright, she snatched the phone off the nightstand where she had dropped it.

"Hello?" She was aware of how her voice sounded and really didn't care.

"Hello, Ms. Spitz, it's Lawrence, Ward's lawyer."

Suddenly she was as awake as if someone had set off an air raid siren next to her. The greeting wasn't lost on her; Ward's lawyer.

"Oh, hello, Lawrence," she managed. "Ward said I would be hearing from you, but he didn't say it would be this soon."

"May I speak to him please? He isn't answering his phone."

Now she was even more awake and confused. "No. He isn't here... isn't that what you're calling me about?"

There was silence on the other end, and Torie thought she heard whispering. She pulled the phone away from her ear enough to see the time on the screen; 7:15. Why would Ward's lawyer be calling her this early? The offices weren't even open until nine.

"Lawrence, what is this about that it can't wait? I'm sure whatever papers you have drawn up don't need to be signed at this hour. Plus, I would like to have my own attorney look over them first." Even though she didn't have an attorney at the moment.

"Ms. Spitz," he started, "Torie. What papers are you talking about?"

"The divorce papers," she said. "Lawrence, what are *you* talking about?"

More silence on the other line. "Torie, I hope you're sitting down. Ward has been involved in running a Ponzi scheme and using his company to funnel the funds. He's liquidated everything that is in both your names and...disappeared." Silence on both ends of the line. "Ms. Spitz are you there? I think we need to talk. Immediately."

## 2

The law offices of Lawrence Tillman were located on the twenty-second floor of a modern, mixed-use building in the hip Chelsea area of Manhattan. There was no denying that he was successful; but as she sat in the posh waiting area, Torie couldn't help but wonder how much of that success was the result of his dealings with her husband.

She resisted the urge to bite her nails, or even worse, smoke a cigarette; a filthy habit she had given up decades ago, before Shawn was born. But she felt like she was a bundle of nerves, strung too tightly and waiting for just the right pick in just the right place before snapping apart.

She could see their lawyer through the open door of his office. He was speaking with someone in a suit and that worried her. No one wore a suit this early in the morning unless they meant business. Even Lawrence was in casual attire, attesting to how quickly he had rushed into his office. He nodded, shook hands with whoever he was speaking with, and escorted the suited man to his office door.

"We'll talk soon," he said, patting the suit on the shoulder. The taller, official-looking man walked past her, nodding slightly before exiting the office.

"C'mon in, Torie," he said, motioning for her to join him in his office.

She entered, and he closed the door behind her, motioning towards the leather couch that sat against one wall, facing a bank of windows that overlooked the Hudson.

"I'd offer you a drink," he said, "but it's a little early."

"I'd take you up on it, but..." she shrugged. Honestly, she didn't care what time it was, but she had the feeling she would need all her wits about her for this conversation.

"First, I'm sorry," he said. "For whatever crappy thing Ward has done and dragged you into. First, you said he told you I was going to reach out to you?"

"Yes. Let me back up. He left me last night. For Wednesday. I assumed when he said you would be in contact that it would be about the divorce papers he had you draw up."

Lawrence shook his head, one hand over his mouth. "He never mentioned anything to me about leaving you."

Torie had stopped trying to figure out what was going on at this point. As soon as she had hung up with Lawrence, she had tried calling Ward on his cell, only to have a recording tell her that the number was no longer in service.

"Yeah, I got the same message," Lawrence said when she told him about the attempted call.

"Lawrence, what is going on? You said something about a Ponzi scheme; and who was that man that was just here?"

He sighed deeply. "That was an FBI agent. One of many that has been assigned to this case. They will be back anytime now with a search warrant to seize my records and..."

"And what?"

"And one for your home, and the apartment here in the city."

Torie felt like someone had knocked the wind out of her for the second time in the last twelve hours.

"What are they looking for?" she asked.

"Anything that can tell them where he is now, and what he's been up to. They're looking for money, Torie. A lot of it. We don't have a lot of time before they come back, so I need you to level with me right here and now; do you know where Ward is?"

She felt the sting of tears in her eyes as she shook her head. "I swear, I have no idea. He told me he was leaving me, we argued, he left; said he couldn't stay in the house. And that was it. What do you know?"

"Just that he took everything. Over the past two weeks he has been moving around money, cashing out accounts."

"Wait, how was he doing all of this without your knowledge? Aren't you his lawyer?"

Lawrence blushed and broke eye contact briefly. "I am his personal lawyer, yes. But his business dealings were handled completely differently."

Something about the way he said that caught Torie's attention. "Lawrence, did you know that he was seeing Wednesday?"

Lawrence took a deep breath, and Torie knew the answer.

"Yes. But he told me he was working things out with you and that it was nothing serious with her. He had her name put on some of the accounts that he moved money into. It wasn't my place to question that. I just made sure that everything was handled appropriately."

"Well, obviously you failed at that." She regretted saying it as soon as the words were out of her mouth. "I'm sorry. That wasn't fair. But... what did you mean by a Ponzi scheme?"

"He would use cooked books to show high return numbers to companies that were thinking about signing on with his company. Then he would take the money they would invest and show it to another company as profits he was making; thus, enticing them to buy in as well. All the while he was using all the money for his own private gains, while not investing any, or very little, into the companies he was swindling. The FBI have been watching him for a while."

"When you say he was using it for private gains...like what?"

"Well, the apartment for one. His cars, the house...all of it."

"Jesus. How long was this going on?"

"According to the FBI, his business was legit originally. This all started when Wednesday came into the picture."

Of course it did. Torie shook her head. One more reason to hate that woman.

"Okay, so what do we do?" she asked.

Lawrence looked at her, an eyebrow arched. "Well, unless you can pay back everything he took from the companies, plus the interest he owes..." He shrugged.

"No, don't shrug at me. I hate the way men do that. Tell me what you mean."

"The FBI will issue a freeze on all assets until this can be settled. And they are putting out an arrest warrant for him. They'll be taking you in for questioning as well. Though it looks like the one thing Ward was careful to do was not implicate you in any of this. The trail he left only points to him."

"So if they freeze everything," she swallowed hard, "how bad is it? Oh God. Shawn's trust."

"Trusts are very difficult to break. They may freeze it, but I don't know if they can take that. But everything else will be fair game."

She nodded, her face going pale. "Everything we...I have?"

"Yes. They will take everything. If you have access to cash, you'll need it. Your credit and equity lines will be frozen immediately."

"How much? How much do we owe?"

He shook his head. "I honestly don't know. It would just be a guess."

"And..."

She nearly fainted at the nine-figure amount he guesstimated.

SHE RETURNED HOME, calling her best friend on the way. All she had to do was tell Freya that she needed her. The tone in her voice conveyed the urgency, and by the time she pulled up to the twelve thousand square foot house, her friend was at the door.

She wasn't the only one that had beat Torie there. She was greeted by the sight of many men and women dressed in black pants and blue jackets that read FBI in yellow block letters across the back.

They were filing in and out of her house, carting out boxes and computers, loading them into black vans that lined her driveway.

As she walked up to the door, before she could even greet Freya, an agent that she recognized from Lawrence's office approached her with a folded piece of paper.

"Ms. Spitz, my name is Jasper Kyle and I have a warrant here to confiscate any and all items in this house that may be considered part of an investigation being run in conjunction with the Treasury Department relating to the business dealings of your husband. Do you know the whereabouts of your husband, ma'am?"

"No. I don't." It was all she could muster as she watched her possessions being manhandled and hauled out of the house.

"Have you had any recent communication with him?" Agent Kyle continued.

She shook her head. "Wait, that's my painting," she pointed to a large canvas work of art that had sat above the mantel in the main living area of the house. "Why are you taking that?"

"We have orders to take any and everything that could have been purchased by illegal means, ma'am."

She was shocked and not sure what to say. "When do I get it back?"

The agent looked at her, his brow furrowed. "That would be up to the courts I'm afraid. Now, if you'll excuse me."

He walked away into the house, giving instructions to the minions that were roaming around there.

Slowly, almost drunkenly, Torie made her way inside accompanied by her best friend.

"My God," said Freya. "Torie, what is going on?"

They would have sat down in the expansive great room, but there was nothing to sit on. The furniture had already been wrapped in plastic and tagged for removal. Instead, they made their way out to the back patio that overlooked the large, immaculately manicured back yard and pool, and sat on the furniture that had not yet been seized. There, Torie told her friend everything she knew.

Freya reached out and took her hand in hers, clasping it tightly. "I am so sorry. I cannot even imagine what you must be feeling right now." She shook her head, her eyes welling up. "That bastard. How could he do this to you and Shawn?"

Freya was a pediatrician and had been Shawn's doctor since childhood. She was one of the few physicians in the wealthy suburb who still made house calls. That was how she and Torie had met all those years ago.

"How are you holding up?" she asked.

"I'm still kind of numb," said Torie. "Last night I thought I was getting a divorce. Today, I find out I've probably lost everything, and my husband is on the run from the FBI."

"Well, don't worry about a place to stay; I've got plenty of room and you don't need to worry about anything right now."

She smiled, thanking her friend for her generosity. The truth was, while she probably shouldn't be alone right now, it was what she was craving.

"And not for nothing, but you know I never fully trusted Ward," Freya said.

"I know," said Torie. Freya had never come right out and bad-mouthed him, but she also had never been a fan either. "The way he kept you locked away here, like you were too precious to do anything other than be his wife and Shawn's mother. One day, Torie, you're going to realize that you can live for yourself, make your own way in this life. And you're going to find someone that appreciates that. You're too good to be someone's prop." Her tone softened and she smiled again. "How's your pain been through all of this?"

Torie sighed. For the past few weeks, she had been suffering considerable cramps, alternating with hot flashes and capped off with bouts of dizziness. When she first told Freya what was happening to her, she was told it was probably perimenopause. Of course, she refused to believe that. She was only forty-five. Didn't the change happen later in life? She had prided herself on eating right, working out constantly in her free time, and being careful not to overdo caffeine and alcohol. Admittedly she could do better on the alcohol front, but come on...she was a middle-aged housewife in suburbia. Drinking was practically a sport.

Had all that sacrifice been for nothing? Here she was, ready for her second act—her son had finally left the nest, her husband had, she thought, a successful business that he would be able to step away from so they could spend more time together; traveling and focusing on themselves, but the universe had other plans for her it seemed. Namely, menopause and destitution.

She turned to her friend and forced a smile. "It's been okay. I think the shock of all this has overwhelmed the hot flashes, and the migraine that I feel coming on is beating off the dizziness. So I think I'll be good." She paused, looking off into the distance. This, her backyard oasis, used to be her fortress of solitude. The quiet calmed her, restored her. Now that was shattered by the intrusive sound of male voices barking orders, and her belongings being dragged out of her home.

She turned to Freya. "Thank you for the offer, but I think I need to stay here. I have to meet with Lawrence later; he's meeting me somewhere in the city so I can give a statement to the FBI and await... whatever they do to women in my position."

Freya offered her own weak smile, then rummaged around in her purse before pulling out a small white pill bottle. She glanced around, then slipped it into Torie's hand. "For later. Just in case you need a little something to help you sleep."

She stood up, still holding her friend's hand. "You call me. Even if you don't want anything, call me to let me know how you're doing. I have a couple of kids to drop in on, but I'll be done in about three hours and will be available anytime thereafter."

Torie stood and hugged her, momentarily afraid to let her go. They parted and Torie sat back on the teak, cushioned chair. With a deep breath, she took out her phone and made the call she had been dreading since Lawrence had told her she would be locked out of her home by the end of the day.

She listened as the other end rang before the line was picked up.

"Hello," she said. "Mom...can we talk?"

# 3

By the end of the day, Torie was exhausted on a level she had never known before. Every inch of her body ached, and her mind was in a fog.

The meetings with the government agencies had been hours of questions; the same ones being asked in different ways, all in an attempt to get her to trip up and spill knowledge she didn't have. Then, after her grand inquisition, came the hard part. She sat through a reading of all the items that had been confiscated by the government.

It would have been quicker to list off what they had let her keep. Lawrence had been right; the house, apartment, artwork, jewelry...all of it was gone. What little money was left in their accounts, the little bit Ward had not taken, was frozen as well. They had taken the cars, leaving her with an older model Infinite sedan that for some reason had been in her name alone. Everything else, however, anything that had both of their names attached, now belonged to the government.

When she had asked Lawrence what would be done with it, he had informed her that more likely than not it would be auctioned off to help pay off Ward's debts. She had managed to get to one of the safes in the New York apartment before the FBI and rescued a couple of thousand dollars in cash, which she stuffed into her purse before the agents entered that part of the house.

Surprisingly, they did not check her person and told her that she could take one bag of clothing with her before they locked up the apartment. She had packed hastily, taking only clothing that were comfortable and would hold up on a long drive.

Then, exhaustion setting in, she had checked herself into a hotel, and promptly fallen asleep on a bed that was nowhere near as comfortable as what she was used to. It didn't matter. She was asleep before her head hit the pillow.

THE NEXT MORNING, she woke up to a headache and a stiffness in her back that caused her to groan with the effort of swinging her legs out of bed. She sat like that, on the edge of the bed, letting her blood pressure settle and the light-headed feeling that had lately taken her over if she got up too fast, to go away. When had all of this happened to her? This old age thing wasn't supposed to hit for another couple of decades she kept telling herself.

She showered and dressed in a pair of jeans and a comfortable sweater that she had grabbed from her old bedroom-sized walk-in closet. Then she headed downstairs to the hotel's dining room for much-needed coffee and some whole wheat toast before heading out to the garage where her car was parked.

Her mind was numb as she eased out into traffic and headed out of the city, merging onto the parkway that would eventually take her to I95 South. She had told Lawrence that she would be heading to her mother's house to stay with her for a while, and after checking with the FBI, he told her that would be fine. They believed she had nothing to do with any of this and were also convinced she truly did not know where Ward was.

She had far bigger worries than Ward. She had called Shawn from Lawrence's office only to be greeted by his cell phone message letting all callers know that he would be pulling an all-nighter in preparation for a major exam. She left him a message telling him to call her right away, that it was important. She wanted him to hear what was going on from her, not read about it online somewhere.

The phone rang just as she was accelerating onto the George Washington Bridge, and she hastily answered it hands free.

"Hello? Shawn?" she said.

"No, babe, it's Freya. I'm just calling to check in on you and let you know that...well, it's out."

Torie swallowed hard. She didn't need to ask what she meant.

"What stations?"

"All of them. Plus, there are news crews swarming your house, waiting like vultures to pick at a carcass."

She felt a pounding in her temples as equal parts embarrassment and anger began to flood her.

"And...well, some of your neighbors are giving...interviews."

Now she was pissed. While she had never been one to welcome her neighbors with open arms, she was never hostile to them either. She donated to their causes, brought generous amounts of cookies and popcorn to support the Scouts, and always threw one massive party every fall to welcome the changing of the seasons. No expenses were spared, and she never complained when the neighbors would eat and drink well into the wee hours of the night.

"Who?" she asked.

"Celinda Jaye, for one."

Of course. That one was always in a non-existent competition with Torie, trying to one up her at every turn. Torie could only imagine how she must be gloating now.

"I'm just telling you because I don't want you turning on the TV and seeing it."

"No worries there. I'm headed out of the city. I'm going down to North Carolina to stay with my mother for a bit until I can figure out what to do."

Her best friend was silent on the other line, and when she finally spoke up, her voice cracked. "Torie, I don't know what to say. I am so sorry this is happening to you. You are one of the strongest, most giving people I have ever known. To see this happen…"

Torie felt her tears begin to flow again. This time, it was her voice that cracked. "Well, it's not like we're never going to see each other again. I just need some time away from this circus. Look, I gotta go; you know I get confused driving on these crazy expressways. I'll call you when I get there."

She hung up and then asked her phone's voice assistant to call Shawn. Again, it went straight to voicemail. She had no idea what class he was studying for or what time his exam was. She left another message and hoped that he would get it prior to receiving a call from any of his old friends that may still live in Westchester. She did a quick calculation of the time difference between New York and Austin and realized that he might not even be in class yet.

She wondered briefly if Ward would try to call him. They were always very close and, while she was surprised that he had walked out on her, it was almost unimaginable that he would leave Shawn without saying goodbye. Thinking about Shawn and how she would explain all of this to him made Torie's blood boil. How could Ward do this to them? What kind of man was he that he thought this was okay?

What kind of woman was she that she had married a man like this? That was a slippery slope to start down. It made her wonder what else he had been hiding from her and for how long. Was their whole relationship a lie? Or was this the fault of his business partner who had sunk her claws into him and filled him with corruption?

No. She may hate Wednesday for her part in this, but Ward was a grown man. *He* was the married one. At some point he had the chance to say no to her; and he had let it pass.

She made the drive, only stopping for gas when needed and the occasional bathroom break. Once she was in Virginia, she started to realize that within a few hours she would be face to face with her mother. She had promised to tell her everything in person rather than when she spoke with her on the phone. That thought was nearly enough to give her another panic attack.

The last time Torie had seen her mother was at Shawn's fifth birthday party. Her mother had been arguing with Ward about something and it had escalated to shouting and name calling. Her mother had told her that Ward was not who he pretended to be and was no good for her. Torie had scoffed at the notion and had taken her husband's side in the fight. Now, looking back, she wondered what had set them off. Ward had said she had started the fight by criticizing him and stating he was not good enough for her daughter.

While that had seemed like something her mother would say, she never got the chance to ask her side of the encounter. The next day, her mother had left before Torie was up. No note was left, no calls returned, and Ward stated that was for the best. The one time they had spoken after that, her mother had asked her if she had left him yet. Torie said she had no intention of leaving him and that she wanted them both in her life, but if it came to a choice, she chose her current family.

Gradually, communication between Torie and her mother grew less and less. Eventually, holiday calls and even birthdays were missed. It had probably been five or six years since they had last spoken. Torie felt her face flush at the thought of that. Her mother was headstrong and direct that was certain; but she was still her mother. Torie wondered how she would feel if she and Shawn didn't speak, and the thought brought pangs to her heart.

Now here she was, forty-five years old and running home to Mama. The thought was almost enough to make her turn around and drive back to New York. She knew she could stay with Freya, but that would mean confronting everyone who knew them in New York and dealing with the media, which she certainly did not want to do.

Torie wasn't stupid. She had seen this exact scenario play out in the media and the court of public opinion involving a much more high-profile society member who had been running the same scheme as her husband. The scandal had destroyed that family. While running from a fight did not sit well with her, she couldn't help but wonder how that high society family might have fared had they opted to disappear from the public.

What would she do if Ward had raided Shawn's trust fund? Or worse, what if the government seized it as an asset? Lawrence was confident they wouldn't be able to; but they were the government. Was there really anything they couldn't do?

She noticed the dying light in the sky as she crossed the border into North Carolina. The sky was streaked with orange and red ribbons against a blue-gray background. The sheer beauty of it was nearly enough to take her mind off her troubles.

She checked the clock and new that she would be in the tiny town of Singing Falls just after nightfall. Her mother had moved there shortly after their fight, and it would be the first time Torie had visited the mountain community. From what she had read online, it was a small arts community nestled in the mountains, and known for the scenic hiking and camping in the summer, and magnificent ski trails in the winter.

The road that her navigation system told her to turn onto was dark, even in the half light, and she found herself slowing down considerably as she crept upward into the mountains; one hairpin turn after the other.

It was a good thing she slowed down, because when she came around one of the curves, she thought she saw a man stagger onto the side of the road. He was bent over, and the beams of her headlights just caught his form. She slammed on the brakes, only to realize no one was there.

But he *was* there; she was sure of that. Had she hit him? Maybe it was her imagination, but she could swear she felt a thump before her car had screeched to a halt.

Without thinking, she climbed out of the car and raced to the front, scanning the area illuminated by her headlights. There was nothing there. Slowly, she made her way to the side of the car.

"Hello? Is anyone there?" She suddenly felt silly, walking around in the near dark looking for someone she may or may not have seen. It had to have been a hallucination. She had been angry and was just thinking of Ward, so maybe her mind projected him in front of her car. Perhaps smashing into him would have been therapeutic in some way, she reasoned.

"Stupid woman," she muttered to herself as she turned to get back into the car.

And that was when she heard it. A weak 'meow' that made its way to her ears. It was faint, and as she stopped to listen, she heard it again, coming from the ditch on the passenger side of the road. The side where she thought she had seen a man stumble out of the shadows.

Following the sound, she saw a small, dark shape huddled in a ball on the side of the road. It purred as she approached, and then meowed in a way that made her think the cat was injured. Badly. Had she hit a cat? God, she hoped not. She looked around, unsure what to do.

Bending down, she reached tentatively for the little fella. "Okay, please don't bite me; I just need to see how hurt you are."

She lightly stroked his fur, felt it stiffen in response when her fingers brushed against its side. The cat had definitely been injured, whether she had done it or not, and it needed care. Looking at her watch, Torie knew she was only about twenty minutes from her mother's house. Surely an arts community would have a vet somewhere in town.

"Okay, I'm going to pick you up. You're coming with me and we are going to get you some help."

She lifted the tiny feline gingerly and eased it into her back seat.

"You're going to be just fine," she said.

The cat, which she could see now was pitch black, sighed deeply and looked at her with large, green eyes. And then, as if it were the most natural thing in the world, it spoke to her.

"Thank you."

# 4

"That's it; I'm losing my mind," Torie said to herself as she made the drive up the winding road to her mother's house. She kept looking at the cat in her rear-view mirror. It was lying in the back seat, eyes closed, breathing in small shallow gasps. For a moment, she considered the bottle of pills Freya had given her, and she wondered just how powerful they were.

Of course they would be for her, not the cat.

Cats don't talk, she kept reminding herself. There was no way that had happened. The stress of the past two days had finally caught up to her and she was now a woman on the verge.

But she had heard it; hadn't she? She knew from watching countless videos on the internet that cats could sometimes sound like they were producing human speech with their vocalizations. But this was different. It was calm and...too human-like. It had said "Thank you" and then seemed to pass out, its head dropping.

Was hearing animals some weird, new menopause symptom? If so, that was all she needed added to the mix.

Even in her shocked state, she still knew the animal needed medical care, so she secured it as best she could with blankets from the trunk and made her way up the mountain.

Her mother's house was a cute, two-bedroom cottage with second-floor dormers that looked like large eyes staring down. It sat back from the winding main road; the front of it dominated by a large porch that spanned the entire length of the house. An actual white picket fence lined the drive to the gravel parking space in front.

Evergreen trees flanked it, towering high above, creating a scenic canopy over the house. Torie could see tendrils of gray smoke wisping out of the chimney. There was a gas lamp post that flickered at the entrance to the sidewalk, illuminating the footpath to the porch. Torie saw a porch light next to the red wooden door flick on as she opened her car door and rushed around to the passenger side back door.

"Torie, is that you?" her mother's voice rang out from the porch.

"Mom? Yes, can you give me a hand? Quickly please."

Her tone told the older woman something was wrong, and she rushed to her daughter's side.

"Torie, what is it? What's going on?"

"I think I hit this cat, Mom." She eased the animal into her arms, turning to give her mother a view.

Her mother gasped, placing one hand over her mouth. "This way, Torie, hurry." She made her way up the path to the house ahead of her daughter.

She ushered Torie into the house, through the great room that dominated the entry, and into a nicely appointed kitchen. Through the kitchen was a back, screened-in patio with a large wooden worktable in the middle of the room.

"Put him here," her mother said, moving an assortment of paint brushes and cans aside to make room on the table.

Gingerly, Torie laid the cat out, still wrapped in the blanket.

Her mother ran into the kitchen and returned almost immediately with a cloth that she had soaked in cold water. She began to carefully dab at the cat's face with the cloth.

"Do you have a vet close by?" Torie asked.

"Not one that will be able to help him. But maybe…" She handed the cloth to her daughter and made her way to a phone on the wall in the kitchen. She dialed a few numbers and spoke in a rushed tone to whoever was on the other end.

When she returned to the worktable, she had a small bottle of water which she slowly poured out into the bottle's cap and tried to get the cat to sip from it.

"Tell me exactly what happened," she said, not looking up at her daughter.

Torie relayed what she remembered, ending with, "I honestly thought I saw a man first. I thought I hit him, but when I got out of the car, I found this little fella."

Her mother snapped to attention, focusing on Torie. "A man? Are you sure?"

"No, Mom, I'm not. That's what I'm saying. It was dark, and the headlights barely caught...whatever it was, in the beam as I came around the corner."

"How did he seem?"

Torie thought for a second. "I don't know. He was kind of staggering; maybe bent forward, but then that was it, he was gone at the same time I slammed on my brakes."

Before anything else could be said, they heard the squeal of tires in the gravel, followed by a car door opening and closing. A half-second later the front door opened, and someone was rushing through the house to join them.

Torie looked up to see two women enter the work room. Both were older, probably the same age as her mother, and dressed in flowing sundresses in vibrant tie-died colors. One woman was tall, with long gray hair that was pulled back in a single long braid that trailed down her back. The other woman was shorter with a stouter build. Her hair was in a natural afro that framed her dark features and striking green eyes.

"Oh my Goddess," said the taller woman, "is that him?"

Torie's mother nodded, trying to coax the cat to drink some water. "Yes. No doubt about it."

Both women rushed to either side of the table, focused on the black cat that laid between them.

"I...I am so sorry," Torie said. "It was dark. I didn't even see him when I came around the curve." Tears began to streak her cheek as she saw the concern on the faces of the women gathered around. She felt terrible, and her stomach began to twist itself into knots.

The shorter woman looked up, almost as if she were seeing her for the first time. "I'm sorry, who are you?"

"This is my daughter, Torie," her mother said. "Torie, this is Fionna and Glen."

Fionna, the darker woman, nodded before turning back to the cat.

"She thinks she hit him with her car. He stumbled out in front of her."

Before Torie could say anything to correct her mother's account of what happened, Glen spoke up.

"What do we do? He can't stay like this. There isn't anything in my medicine bag that will help him in this condition," she said.

"We called Ellie on the way over. She's on her way," said Fionna. Both women exchanged glances before looking at Torie's mother. "She was down in Trinity. She's grabbing a few items and heading right up."

"That means she's at least an hour away," said Torie's mother. "We need to make sure he stays alive until she gets here." She looked at her confused daughter. "Ellie is a special kind of vet. She's not from around here..."

That made Torie feel slightly better, but she could tell from the concern around her that the women thought the cat might not make it until then.

"What can I do?" she asked.

"Stay out of the way," said Fionna, her voice little more than a snarl. She softened immediately after seeing the hurt look on Torie's face. "I'm sorry. I didn't mean that. Here, come with me, we need to brew a special tea that will help him."

She took Torie by the hand, gave a quick look in Glen's direction, and dragged her into the kitchen. Once there, she rummaged through the cabinets until she found a small pot. Handing it to Torie, she told her to fill it halfway with water and put it on the stove to boil.

Torie did as she was told, setting the gas range to high to hasten the boil.

"I really am sorry. I didn't mean to hit your cat," she said.

Fionna regarded her, cocking her head to one side. "He isn't our cat. At least, not in the way you think."

Now it was Torie's turn to be confused. "But...I mean, the way you are both acting. I assumed he belonged to you."

Fionna threw back her head and laughed. "If he survives, he will get quite the kick out of what you just said."

Torie frowned. The way this woman was speaking about the cat reminded her of what she had not told her mother about the encounter.

"You make him sound almost human," said Torie.

"Almost," replied Fionna, her voice soft and silky.

She continued her rummaging, this time going through the upper cabinets until she found what she was looking for. Removing a small, silver container from a middle shelf, she brought it to the large island that sat in the middle of the space. Then she quickly went to another cabinet and took out a marble mortar and pestle. She opened the container and emptied the contents into the mortar.

Torie caught a whiff of sage and thyme, and another smell that she could not place. Fionna began grinding the green spices, mashing them into a fine grain.

"As soon as the water boils, bring it over," she said.

No sooner had the words been spoken than Torie noticed the bubbles breaking the surface of the water. She grabbed the pot and brought it to Fionna.

"Good," said the older woman, "now, slowly pour it into the mortar as I grind. Slowly, I only need a small amount to make a paste."

Torie did as she was told, careful not to burn the strange woman who was intent on working the mixture. The water hit the herbs, giving off a slightly pungent odor that surprised Torie. As she ground the mixture into a sticky, almost waxy consistency, Fionna began to chant lightly under her breath; so lightly that Torie could not make out what she was saying.

She didn't get the chance to ask. The older woman picked up the mortar and motioned for Torie to follow her back into the work room.

"This may help until Ellie can get here," she said, placing the mixture on the table next to the cat. Dipping her fingers in the paste, she applied a dollop to the cat's side and began massaging it in. To Torie's surprise, the cat meowed loudly and began to stir.

Torie looked at her mother who was standing, one hand covering her face, the other clasping Glen's. The look on their faces surpassed worry, it was as if they were watching a friend in extreme pain.

"Mom," said Torie, "whose cat is this?"

Her mother looked at her and shook her head. "He doesn't belong to anyone. He is our friend."

Torie frowned. Obviously, her mother was clearly upset, but it didn't explain this type of action. She hadn't looked this upset when Torie's father had died all those years ago. For so long she had thought her mother was made of ice; but this behavior was the opposite of everything Torie remembered about her.

She watched as Fionna finished applying the rub to the cat's body. It had stopped mewling and seemed to be sleeping again. Glen stepped forward and stroked its head.

"You're going to be okay," she whispered through tears. "Can you hear me? We're all here with you. You're not alone, and we all need you to fight. Just hold on…Ellie is coming."

Something about the level of care, no, love, in her voice, caused Torie to speak up.

"I think…I mean, I thought, that he spoke to me." Her eyes were locked on the animal on the table. She didn't want to see the look of judgment that she figured her mother was giving her.

"What?" said her mother, "he spoke to you? Why didn't you say so?"

"What did he say?" asked Fionna, her eyes frantic as she searched Torie's face.

Whatever reaction Torie thought she would get from them, this was certainly not it. She cleared her throat. "He said, thank you."

They were quiet before Glen spoke up. "What did you say to him before he spoke?"

"Something like…it's going to be okay, I'm going to get you help, or something like that."

"What else did he say?" said Glen. "It's important that you tell us everything."

"That was it, I swear. I mean, I'm sure I imagined that much. Didn't I? Cats don't talk. Right?" She wasn't sure what was real anymore. She wanted a drink, or a Vicodin. Or both. Christ, where was Freya when she needed her?

The three women exchanged looks, and finally her mother came around to her side of the table and took her hand.

"Torie, we have a lot to talk about. I'm not sure now is the right time, however."

"Why not?" asked Fionna. "If he spoke to her, it was for a reason. If he dies…"

"He isn't going to die," said Glen, her eyes focused on the cat. "He just can't."

"Mom, what is going on here? Do you actually believe that a cat talked to me?"

"He's not just a cat," her mother replied. "He's a shifter. And right now, he's locked in his feline form. He was attacked, and if Ellie doesn't get here soon to save him, he's going to die. Just like the rest of them."

## 5

Torie looked at her mother like she had grown a second head.

"What are you talking about? What's a shifter?" she asked.

"A shifter is a human that is capable of taking on the form of an animal," her mother replied. "There are many of them in this area. Cats, foxes, deer; all manner of shifter."

"This particular shifter is named Eddie. He's a friend," said Fionna, reaching over to rub the cat's head lovingly.

Now it was Torie's turn to wonder if her mother had lost her marbles. She had always been a little out there, but this was pushing it.

"Mom, are you okay? Listen to what you're saying."

Her mother looked at her incredulously. "The nerve of you to come here after making it a point to be out of my life for fifteen years…to come here into my house and tell me I don't know what I'm saying about my friends."

Torie felt like she had been stung. She realized how she must have sounded, but she wasn't sure how else to respond to what she had just been told.

"I don't mean any disrespect," she said, "it's just...I mean, what you're saying...it makes no sense."

"It will in time," said her mother, reaching out to take Torie's hand. "It's a lot, and I promise you, I will tell you everything. But right now, we need to take care of Eddie."

Suddenly, a shadow crossed her features and her face became a mask of worry. She rushed to the window in the front of the house and looked out carefully before drawing the blinds shut.

"What is it?" asked Torie, clearly on edge now.

"Did you see anyone else?" asked her mother.

"No. I mean, I don't think so."

Fionna and Glen looked at one another, clearly worried about something. Torie felt like the outsider looking in, which of course she was at this point, but she also felt like there was something going on that she clearly needed to know about.

"What is it?" she asked everyone in the room.

Glen took a deep breath. "You didn't hit Eddie with your car. This was a deliberate attack on him."

"How do you know?" said Torie.

"Because I can feel the wound," said Fionna. She stretched out a hand, letting it hover a few inches over Eddie's feline body. "Here, in his side. He was stabbed; with a magical instrument."

Fionna walked around to Torie, placing a hand on her arm. "Someone...some*thing*, attacked Eddie. Tried to kill him."

Torie's mind was swimming. "Why would someone do that?"

"The shifters in Singing Falls are being hunted and murdered," said Torie's mother, her voice sounded strained and tired. "We don't know by who or why."

"We think it's a supernatural serial killer," said Fionna.

Torie wasn't sure how to respond. Her first instinct was to laugh, but she kept that in check. She really needed a big glass of wine. Maybe she was dreaming. Had she hit her head on the steering wheel? Was she still in her car unconscious? She wrapped her arms around her body and gave herself a squeeze.

No. She felt real; just trapped in an unreal place at the moment.

That would explain the fact that she was sure she saw a man...No. She shook her head. She was sleep deprived; none of this was happening.

"Mom, I don't know what is going on here, but—"

"Oh, we don't have time for this," said her mother. "Fionna?"

Torie turned to face Fionna, just in time to see the taller woman suddenly shrink; her form twisting and transforming in the blink of an eye. Where just a second before a grown woman had stood, in her place was a small, silver squirrel. The squirrel sat up on her hind legs before once again twisting and growing back into her human form.

Torie stared at her, then at Glen, and finally her mother. She raised a hand lazily to point at Fionna, but before she could find her words, darkness crowded in and she collapsed onto the cool, wood floor.

SHE AWOKE ON THE COUCH, relishing the feel of a cold compress on her forehead. Her head felt full of cobwebs, like she had succumbed to one too many glasses of cheap red wine. She sat up gingerly, sorting out her surroundings and the voices she was hearing.

"Take it easy," said Fionna. She was sitting on the coffee table next to the couch Torie sat on. "I think you might have smacked your head when you fainted." She reached out to touch her, and Torie jerked back as if she were about to be scalded. Fionna smiled, masking the hurt she felt, and withdrew her hand.

"What...what are you?" Torie asked.

"A shifter. Squirrel shifter. I'm sorry you had to find out that way, but your mother was right. With Ellie on her way, we wouldn't have been able to take the time to explain things to you and provide Ellie whatever help she may have needed with Eddie." Fionna stood, offering her hand to Torie to assist her in getting to her feet. "Besides, it was only a matter of time before you found out everything anyway."

Torie stood, thankful for the other woman's support as she was a little shaky on her feet. Before she could ask Fionna what she meant by that, she heard multiple voices coming from the workroom.

"Who's that?" she asked.

"Come on," said Fionna. "That's Ellie, the vet. She arrived just after you passed out."

Torie followed her through the kitchen and back into the room that her mother had been using as a makeshift art studio and had now been transformed into an animal clinic.

"Aw, there she is," said Glen. "You feeling okay?"

Torie nodded, pressing the compress she still held against the back of her head. She nodded to the new person in the room.

"Ellie?" she said, extending a hand, "I'm Torie, Alva's daughter."

"Yes, I know who you are. Word spreads fast. Nice to meet you, Torie," said Ellie. Torie frowned. It was a strange feeling; meeting someone that seemed to already know who you were.

"Uh, how's Eddie?" Torie asked.

The veterinarian frowned, turning her attention to the black cat on the table. He seemed to be sleeping, his breathing far more regular than the last time Torie had looked at him. One of his paws was wrapped in a white bandage with a tiny tube peeking out that was connected to an IV bag hanging from a hook on the wall behind the table head.

"He's stable," Ellie said. "It's going to be touch and go for a while. Of course, if it weren't for you he would be dead by now. Thank you for bringing him in."

Torie nodded. She wasn't used to being thanked for doing what any decent person should have done. She took the moment to study Ellie. While Torie had no preconceived idea of what a veterinarian should look like, she was pretty sure it wasn't this. Ellie was short, and to use something she once heard Shawn say, stacked. Torie could not have guessed her age; she had black hair that was streaked with silver highlights, hazel eyes, and skin that was weathered from a lifetime spent in the sun.

But her energy was unmistakable. She practically hummed with pent-up energy. Her speech patterns were just a tad too fast, and she buzzed from place to place. Even when she was standing still, her hands were in motion, fingers curling and uncurling. She smiled at Torie in a genuine, accepting kind of way; another thing Torie wasn't used to coming from the suburbs of New York City.

"So, what now? Should we take him to a hospital?" Torie asked.

Ellie shook her head. "They wouldn't know what to do with him. No, he's better off here, at least until he's stable enough to shift back to his human form."

"The way Fionna did? Why can't he just turn human and then you can take him to the hospital?"

"Because he was stabbed in his human form. The attacker used a blade that was coated in something that we have yet to identify. Something that is lethal to shifters. The blade pierced his skin but not deep enough to hit an artery or internal organ. He must have fought the attacker off and ran away."

"He made it to the main road, which was where you found him," said Alva.

Ellie nodded. "And like I said, that's a good thing. He must have been passing out and instinctively shifted into his feline form. It's what's keeping him alive."

"How is that keeping him alive?" Torie asked.

"Our animal forms are far more resilient than our human ones," said Fionna. "Like most of nature, we aren't quite as susceptible to the kinds of things that humans are."

"Like whatever poison was used on this blade," said Ellie. "The other victims all died before they could shift into animal form. But for some reason, Eddie was able to get away and shift."

There was a black bag sitting on the table next to Eddie, and Torie watched as the veterinarian walked over to it and retrieved a syringe. She then inserted it into the catheter tip of the cat's IV and withdrew a sample of blood.

Holding it up to the light, she studied it closely. "This is also the first chance we've had to get a blood sample of the toxin. Usually it burns itself out, leaving no trace. But it's still active in Eddie...he's fighting it with everything he has. Hopefully I can get this to a lab down in Trinity and we can figure out what we are up against."

"And who's doing this," added Glen.

Torie's mind was swimming with the flood of questions she longed to ask. But she didn't feel like she was in any position to question what was going on. After what she had just seen, she certainly believed her mother. In fact, she was terrified at the thought of what it might mean that her mother was in such a close friendship with these shifters. Why would they have adopted her into their midst?

"So, what about Eddie?" Torie asked. "Does he just stay here like this?"

"For now, yes," replied Ellie. "He's too unstable to move."

"We will take care of him," said Alva, looking at her daughter. "I'll call you if there is any change at all. In the meantime, you two go home and get some rest." She glanced at Glen and Fionna. "And remember; there is safety in numbers."

Ellie packed her bag and embraced Alva before turning to walk out. "Seriously, call me if there is any change at all. I'll go down to Trinity, drop this off and head right back up." The door closed softly behind her, leaving only Fionna and Glen.

"You be careful too," said Glen, as she gave Torie's mother a hug.

"Call us," said Fionna, giving Alva a hug as well. She turned to Torie. "It was nice to meet you, Torie. I hope we can be great friends." Then she gave her a hug and a smile and left the room with Glen.

When they were alone, Torie looked from Eddie to her mother, a million questions dancing across her face.

Alva sighed deeply as she turned to her daughter. "C'mon, let's put some tea on and we can talk. I guess we have a lot to catch up on." She took one last look at Eddie, noted that he was resting comfortably, and then escorted her daughter into the kitchen.

She filled a blue-gray kettle with water and placed it on the gas range to boil. Torie said nothing, watching her mother set about taking down cups and an impressive selection of tea from her cupboards.

"Mom, what is going on here? How do you know these people?"

Her mother smiled. "These people are my people; and they're yours now as well."

"What do you mean?"

Her mother didn't say anything, but instead went about taking the kettle off the stove and steeping the tea. She took out honey, sugar and milk, indicating that her daughter should fix it the way she wanted. Once they each had a steaming cup in hand, they retired to the living room and sat on the couch.

"Torie, this town, this community, is comprised of supernaturals. By that I mean fairies, shifters, witches, the occasional ghost or two... and everyone here lives in peace and harmony. No one wants any trouble with the outside world. But about six months ago, trouble found Singing Falls. There was a murder. A deer shifter was found decapitated. Then, a few weeks later, another shifter was found, cut open with his heart removed." She swallowed hard, taking a tentative sip of her tea before she continued. "It's happened regularly since then. Someone is hunting the shifters in the community. And I'm terrified that if they aren't stopped soon, the shifters may not be the only paranormal creatures hunted."

Torie sipped her tea as well. "Mom, why are you here, living among them?"

"Because, Torie, I am a witch. And so are you."

## 6

After everything that Torie had seen, she shouldn't have been shocked by what her mother just said.

"Oh, for God's sake, Mom," she said. "Witches? What, were goblins already taken?"

Her mother's eyes grew large and her hand flew to her mouth. "Torie, don't joke about goblins; nasty creatures, those little things."

Torie stared incredulously. Her mother was being serious. "I don't even know what to say."

"Well, there really isn't much for you to say. I guess it's up to me to keep telling you what's going on." She smoothed back her auburn hair, the same hair that she had passed onto her daughter. "You heard me right, we are witches. So was my mother and her mother before her. It runs in our family."

Torie looked at her mother, trying to gauge just how serious she was.

"What?" said her mother, "you just saw a grown woman turn into a squirrel, and I promise you that is nothing compared to what some of the townspeople here can do." She could tell that her daughter was having a hard time believing her; despite the evidence before her own eyes. "Fine." She looked around the room and pointed at a set of candles on the fireplace mantle.

Torie's eyes looked like saucers when the candles ignited, the flames shooting a couple of feet high before settling down to their normal burn.

Next, her mother picked up her cup of tea, stood up, still holding it in her hands, and then let it go. Rather than crash to the floor, it floated in mid-air, perfectly balanced. Torie stood up and examined the cup, waving her hands over and under it in wonder.

"How?"

"Low level telekinesis was a gift of my magic. The fire is an incantation I learned. A way to harness the energy around me and use it as I see fit. Like I said, we are witches."

Torie flopped down on the coffee table. "When did this start?"

Her mother smiled. "Not until I was in my forties. The same age as you, my dear."

"Are you saying...are you saying this is going to happen to me? That I could start burning things or whatever?"

"Maybe."

"Wait, what do you mean maybe? You just said we are witches and then you..." She pointed to the candles.

"Witches have various types of gifts, Torie. Not all of them can do the same things. Who knows how your craft will present itself."

Torie's mind was swimming. She wasn't sure what to make of what she had just learned. She was definitely beyond doubting at this point. Granted, for a moment, part of her wanted to believe that her mother had somehow staged this and was pulling a fast one on her, but she knew that wasn't true.

"How did you learn what you could do?" Torie asked.

"Well, one day, I was having the worst migraine. I had always suffered from them, but they increased when I started going through the change. I woke up one morning with one, it was so bad, all I could see was flashes of light, and it felt like someone was using my head as a pin cushion. So, I made it to the bathroom and took some Excedrin, went back to bed and crawled under the covers. Only I had forgotten to draw the curtains tight. The sun came streaming in and it felt like the pain behind my eyes went from ten to one hundred all at once.

"Well, I remember lying there and thinking my head was going to explode if someone didn't shut that curtain, but I couldn't move. And then, just like that—" she snapped a finger, "the curtains shut. Just whipped shut in the blink of an eye. At the same time, the pain in my head started to go away. I was so wiped out that I must have passed out. I woke up a couple of hours later feeling much better and thinking I had dreamed the whole thing. But I didn't, and what's more, after that moment, if I concentrated hard enough, I could move things with my mind. Little things at first, but the more I practiced, the more I could do. That was how it all started."

She looked at her daughter, waiting for a response.

"Why didn't you tell me?"

"Baby, at that time I didn't know what was going on. I had no clue about these things. I did what anyone would do back then."

"Went to a doctor?"

"What? No way. I went to the library. We didn't have the Internet back then, so I had to research things the old-fashioned way. I found a book on strange phenomena and unexplained outbreaks of psychic events. The more I looked, the more I found. Most of it was just new age nonsense, but I did find a work that focused on older women developing powers and abilities later in life. I read every word of it, then tracked down the author. She lived in Charlottesville and when I finally found her, she was the one who told me about witchcraft and how it most likely was passed down in my family."

That got Torie's attention. "Did you talk to Gram about this?"

Her mother shook her head, her eyes growing misty. "We didn't have the best relationship. She wasn't really in the picture at the time, and well, once I thought about flying out west to talk to her about it... it was too late. The funny thing is, she had a connection to this town as well. But more on that later."

Torie didn't say anything. She remembered that her grandmother wasn't really in the picture when she was growing up. What memories she did have of the older woman were fuzzy at best. She looked at her own mother, a pang of longing hitting her square in the chest. There was a moment of silence that passed between them, and in that moment, more was conveyed than they had spoken about in ten years.

"I'm sorry that things between us got bad, Mom."

Her mother patted her hand before giving it a squeeze. "Hush. We don't need to go backwards. You're here now, and judging from the look of things, just as you are coming into your own power."

Torie was taken aback. "What do you mean? What power?"

"Well, I don't know what it will be or what it is called, but you said that Eddie in there spoke to you when he was in his cat form, right?" Torie nodded. "Well, I can't understand shifters when they aren't in their human form; as far as I know, no one can."

A swath of cold wetness broke out on Torie's back. "Wait, you mean they don't speak when they are animals?"

"Not that I know of. They can communicate with one another, but not with humans. They certainly don't speak in complete English sentences."

Shock spread across Torie's features and her body went rigid. "Are...are you saying I'm a shifter?" For some reason the thought terrified her.

Her mother laughed. "No. Now *that* I highly doubt. Supernatural creatures are born that way. I'm not a shifter, so neither are you."

"So then what does that make me?"

Alva shrugged, giving her daughter a playful smile. "Like I said, our gifts can be different. There are a couple of other witches around. I can introduce you to them tomorrow. Maybe they will have an idea. But first, we need to keep an eye on Eddie tonight."

Her brow furrowed as a scary thought crossed Torie's mind. "Do you think the killer might come here?"

"No. That I doubt. I just meant we need to watch him to make sure he doesn't get worse until Ellie can get him back on his feet again."

The mention of the vet's name triggered questions for Torie. "Hey, so I get it that Fionna is a shifter, but what is Glen? And Ellie?"

"They're both human. Nothing magical about them."

"So why is Glen hanging around Fionna then?"

Her mother looked at her, arching an eyebrow.

"Oh," said Torie, suddenly embarrassed she hadn't considered it. "They make a cute couple."

"Yes, they do," agreed Alva.

"So, Mom, how did you end up here in Singing Falls? I always wondered what made you choose this town to relocate."

"Ah, well, after I tracked down that author in Charlottesville, she told me about a tiny community up in the mountains of North Carolina that I might want to visit. She didn't tell me why, just that I should take a look at it. I did that and immediately fell in love with the place. It felt like home the minute I set foot here. And of course, I was welcomed with open arms."

"They knew you were a witch?"

Alva nodded. "Like knows like. Long story short, I sold the house you grew up in and moved here. This became my home, and I will never leave it. These people became my family; and that's why I am determined to help find whoever is killing shifters and dish out some justice served cold." Her eyes grew hard in a way that Torie had never seen.

But then, just as quickly, they refocused on her daughter and filled with warmth. "But that's not what we should be talking about, is it?"

Torie felt herself blush as she tried to figure out how to tell her mother what she had been through. Finally, she opted to just tell her exactly what had happened. Everything came out in a rush; a cleansing outpouring of what had happened from the awkward conversation at the dinner table with Ward, to the arrival in North Carolina and her thinking she had run over a man-cat shifter type.

Her mother said nothing, but instead walked into the room where Eddie was still sleeping on the table, covered up with a soft blanket. Satisfied there had been no change, she headed back into the kitchen. She started to reach for the tea kettle, but then thought better of it.

Torie sat on one of the bar chairs at the island and watched as her mother opened the door of a large bookcase that sat on one of the walls in the kitchen. She took out two low-ball tumblers and a bottle of Carolina Whiskey. A couple of two finger pours later, she clinked glasses with her daughter and pulled up a chair next to her.

"I am so sorry, Torie," she said, her voice warm and comforting. "I know you loved your life."

Something in her tone stopped Torie mid-drink. "What do you mean by that?"

"Nothing. Just that you have a great life. This is a setback."

"I don't think that's what you meant. You never cared for my life. You certainly never cared for Ward."

Her mother's eyes narrowed, and she gave a slight snort as she returned to her whiskey, swirling the amber liquid before taking another swallow.

"Mother, that day at Shawn's birthday party; what happened between you and Ward?" She had never come right out and asked before. They had talked around it, but she only knew what Ward had told her.

Alva sat her drink down and swiveled to face her daughter. "Okay, you want to know? I'll tell you. I told you before that man was not right for you. I'm betting right about now you're wishing you had listened."

Torie winced at that, and Alva was instantly sorry for what she said.

"I'm sorry. I didn't mean that. But he was not a good person. You know, I had found my power by then, and I could see the darkness in him; his aura was all muddy and smoky. He was hiding a lot from you, and I was afraid for your safety and Shawn's. I confronted him, wanted to know what he was up to and hiding. Something in his eyes told me he knew I knew something was up. He told me if I knew what was good for me I'd mind my business."

Torie gasped, her hand starting to tremble at the recounting.

"I told him I wasn't afraid of him and that I was going to talk to you and warn you about him. He told me that wasn't a good idea.

Now, he didn't come right out and threaten you; and he never said a cross thing about Shawn, but he did intimate that if things got bad between the two of you, I would most likely never see you again; that he'd have to disappear..." her voice cracked and she fought back tears, "that what little relationship you and me had would be over just like that.

"I looked into his soul and saw that he meant every word he said. How he would do it I didn't know, but I did know that me hanging around would be bad for you and my grandson. So, I left. Decided to make my new life here that very day."

Torie shook her head slowly, sadness threatening to overwhelm her. "I am so sorry, Mom. I had no idea. He seemed so...so perfect."

"Well he wasn't. He was a schemer that one. And I didn't know how much he was already in your head. I trusted that things would work out by the time you went through your change; that you'd be with me to guide you. And here you are. Of course, I also hoped that you would have a little girl by now too, someone to continue our legacy. But once I realized that he couldn't have any more children, I knew that wouldn't be happening."

"Wait, what are you talking about? How did you know I can't have any more children?"

It was a secret heartbreak that she had never confided to anyone other than Ward, and hearing her mother mention it so casually pained her to her core.

Alva frowned, studying her daughter. "You? No, child, it isn't you. He had something done that altered the natural flow of life-giving essence in his body. I could see it." Her gaze grew distant as she stared at Torie. "Once you master your craft, you'll see people for who they really are as well."

"A vasectomy," Torie whispered. She remembered that time when he had taken a few days off from work because he had hurt himself at the gym playing basketball; or so he said. The bastard had laid around the house with ice on his crotch while she dutifully made him sandwiches and brought him drinks.

Torie didn't say anything, opting instead to down the last of her whiskey in a single gulp before pouring another. This time, she refused to cry. She thought back to a particularly painful conversation where they had been trying and trying to have another child and Ward had finally convinced her it just wasn't in the cards. He had hinted that maybe, just maybe, she was out of the child-bearing age and it was probably for the best.

She had hated her own body for a while, and he had let her.

No, this time she would not cry, because she wasn't hurt. She was angry. And somehow, some way, she intended for him to feel some pain too.

# 7

The next morning was a slow one for them. Mother and daughter had spent the majority of the night sitting up and watching Eddie while nursing the bottle of whiskey.

Alva showed her daughter more of the magic she possessed, explaining how she never really felt alive until her powers had opened up. Torie listened, enraptured by the description her mother gave of how she now saw the world. She reassured her daughter that her time was definitely coming, but there wasn't much she could do to actually teach her the ways of magic.

There were certain individuals that were far more versed in teaching than Alva, and she had promised to introduce Torie to them soon. The night had passed quickly with them; they laughed easily as they caught up on fifteen years of silence. The whiskey went down way too smoothly, and Torie didn't have the strength to refuse when her mother insisted she turn in and get some shut eye.

The guest bedroom was comfortable and well-appointed, and for the first time in days, Torie had woken up without the lingering pains, both physical and mental, that had become like old friends to her.

She walked into the kitchen to find her mother speaking with

Fionna. The taller woman was making a pot of very strong-smelling coffee.

"Hello, Torie," she said, "I made extra, because judging from the shape this one is in, I imagined you could use some caffeine as well."

Torie whispered a grateful thank you as Fionna poured a scalding cup of the brew and handed it to her.

"How is he?" Torie asked.

"Doesn't seem to be any change," said Alva. "Ellie will be back soon to check in on him."

"I came over to give you two a break and keep an eye on Eddie," said Fionna. "I figured you could use some down time to catch up, but," she eyed the empty bottle on the island, "looks like you got that covered."

"Why don't you two head into town and get some of those delicious carrot cake muffins at Jim's?" said Alva. "I need to shower, straighten up around here a little anyway. I'll wait for Ellie, see what she knows."

"Oh, Mom, no. I'll stay and help."

"I will not have that," said Alva. "You go. I want you to see the town. Fionna, take her to that breakfast clutch you have, or whatever you call it; introduce her to some of the girls. I've a feeling she could do with making some new friends."

"Sure," said Fionna. "And it's just a breakfast club, Alva...not a clutch." She looked at Torie, smiling. "You up for meeting some of the crazy town folk that call this place home?"

Torie looked around, questioning her mother. "I mean, if you're sure you're okay here by yourself?"

"Oh, go on...get out of here. I may be old, but I'm not elderly. I'll be fine. Besides, Ellie will be here anytime now."

"Alright," said Torie. "Let me grab a jacket then and I'll be right back." She hurried to her room, checked her hair once in the mirror, before grabbing her jacket and heading back to the living room.

Before she headed out the door with Fionna, she turned and walked to her mother.

"Thank you for last night." She hugged her tightly. "You have no idea how good that felt."

Her mother gave her a squeeze before shooing her out of the kitchen. She stepped outside to see Fionna waiting in a BMW convertible with the top down.

"Nice ride," she said, climbing in the passenger side.

"Thank you," Fionna replied. "It's a bit flashy. But then, I can be too."

They laughed as Fionna eased out of the gravel drive and gunned the car heading for the heart of the tiny town. The drive in was scenic and beautiful. The crisp mountain air did wonders for Torie's hangover. The sun came in and out of view, an ever changing, dappled pattern as it broke through the overhead trees that lined the road.

"Where's Glen?" asked Torie.

"She's on days at the hospital this week. She's a nurse anesthetist, so long hours."

Torie nodded. "I'm sorry if I seemed a little off last night. I wasn't really feeling myself, and everything that was thrown at me just... well, it was a shock."

"I can imagine. It's not every day that you find out that supernatural creatures actually exist."

Since she cracked that window a bit, Torie took it upon herself to open it wide. "So, you didn't acquire your ability to turn into a squirrel? You were born this way?"

"I was. Both of my parents were squirrel shifters, so I really didn't have a choice in the matter."

"Are all supernatural creatures born that way?"

Fionna nodded. "Only witches grow into their powers from what I know. The rest of us are what we are from birth. Though I guess you could say the same for witches. You just get your powers later in life. Was Alva able to tell you what your power will be?"

"No, not really. She said she wasn't sure, but that it had something to do with my ability to hear what Eddie was saying when he was in his feline form."

"That is rare. I have heard of other supernaturals who could hear the thoughts of shifters, but I've never met a human witch who would speak to them."

"Can you speak to one another when you're shifted?"

"Usually, yes. There are exceptions to every rule, however."

"Like what?" Torie asked.

"Well, if we communicate as soon as we shift, it's easier. But the longer we stay in animal form, the harder it can get to communicate with a different species of shifter. The longer we stay in our animal forms, the more animal-like we become."

Torie swiveled to look at Fionna more closely. "You mean, you become the animal inside as well as out?"

"Something like that. There are some in our community that choose to live as their animal selves totally. They never shift back to human form. I've heard that if you spend too much time in animal form, you can forget how to shift back."

"Fascinating," said Torie. "Well, I hope you never decide to do that. It would be a shame to lose the first friend I've made in a long time."

She looked around as they pulled onto the town's main street. It was quaint, and Torie fell in love with it immediately. There were beautiful Victorians with large porches and elaborate signs on them advertising what kind of businesses they were. Brick and stone buildings also lined the space. They were connected three in a row with each having its own unique personality. There were angled parking slots in front of each of the structures, and Fionna eased her two-seater into one of them.

As they climbed out, Torie noticed there were no parking meters to be seen, and she wondered briefly how the town paid to keep up the lush landscaping and picturesque brick sidewalks that were lined with gas lamps, their flames flickering even in the brightness of morning.

"Come on," said Fionna, "Jim's Best Bakery is right up here. You'll love it."

They walked up the sidewalk to a very pretty, white Victorian with blue trim and shutters. Torie's stomach growled at the smells that were coming from the building. The growls turned into full-blown roars when Fionna opened the door and ushered her inside.

The space was beautifully appointed with comfortable leather chairs in small seating groups with round coffee tables between them. There was a large, glass display case that ran along one wall, leading to the cash register that had an elaborately painted 'Order Here' sign attached to it.

Torie didn't have to wonder if everything was home-made—nothing from a box or a microwave could possibly have smelled so heavenly. She lingered at the display case, marveling at the assortment of croissants, pastries, breakfast sandwiches and more. If this had existed in Westchester, she would not have given it a second thought; eating sweets like this would have been out of the question. God forbid someone had seen her munching so much as a donut. The thought of it would have driven her to the gym for a couple of hours at least.

But here, in this tiny town, she felt like she was finally free of that old mindset and couldn't wait to try one of everything.

A small, swinging door behind the counter opened and a man in a white apron and a pastry chef hat stepped up, greeting them both.

"Well hey there, Fionna. Long time no see," he said.

Fionna smiled, shaking her head. She turned to Torie and said, "That's his way of saying I was just in here yesterday."

"And I never get tired of seeing you, my dear. The usual?"

"Yes, please. Two if you don't mind. This is my new friend Torie. She's Alva's daughter."

The gentleman smiled and nodded slightly to her. "Very pleased to meet you, Torie. You are welcome in here anytime."

Torie smiled as Fionna led her to the front of the bakery where there was a set of leather, wing-backed chairs arranged around a table in front of a large double window overlooking the sidewalk. There were two other women sitting there, engaged in animated conversation.

"Fionna!" exclaimed one, standing to greet the two women. "I didn't think you would be here today." She leaned over and hugged Fionna warmly.

"I wasn't either, but here I am. Jasmin, this is my friend Torie. This is Alva's daughter. She just arrived from New York."

"Nice to meet you, Torie," said Jasmin, reaching out to shake hands. "Come, sit with us."

Torie smiled as the second of the women got up to drag another chair into their circle, motioning for her to have a seat.

"Torie, these are my friends; Taylor and Jasmin, whom you just met. The three of us typically have breakfast and coffee here every morning," said Fionna. "They are just about the best friends a woman could ask for."

"Well, I'm betting Fionna has talked your ear off, Torie, but you're still here so that means I like you already," said Taylor. They all laughed, even Fionna, at the light-hearted jab. It was just what Torie needed to break the ice.

"Hey, Fi," said Jasmin, "how is Eddie? We were just discussing that when you walked up."

Fionna sighed deeply. "He's stable, but in very bad shape. He's locked in his animal form while he heals. Ellie thinks it's best that he stay that way. Surely he would be dead by now had he remained human."

They all shook their heads collectively.

"This is terrible," said Jasmin. "Someone has to do something. You're all being hunted."

"Oh," said Fionna, "Torie is the one that found him and brought him to Alva's. Just in time." She leaned into the group and lowered her voice. "He spoke to Torie, after shifting to a cat; and she understood him."

Their eyes widened as they turned to look at the newcomer in their midst.

"So...you're a witch then?" said Taylor. She had long, blonde hair and high cheekbones. She was dressed in a pair of stylish denim jeans and a white tee shirt with a scooped neck. Her leather jacket set the entire look off just right, and Torie couldn't help but think she would fit right in at any New York get-together.

"I suppose," said Torie. "Maybe. Still not sure about that."

They nodded.

"Yes, I guess it can be confusing when your gifts first start to appear," said Jasmin, brushing a stray strand of black hair out of her eyes. Like the other women, she was probably in her late forties and dressed in a nice, yellow sun dress that complimented her dark skin. She wore a large white belt cinched around her waist, and cowboy boots added a touch of whimsy to her outfit. Something about the twinkle in her eyes put Torie instantly at ease.

Torie's eyes lit up. "Wait, are you a witch as well?"

Jasmin smiled and nodded. "I am. Nice to meet another sister."

"And you?" asked Torie, turning to face Taylor.

"I'm a fox shifter. So not a member of your select sisterhood." She smiled to let Torie know it was all in good fun.

"We are all sisters here," said Fionna.

"Are you all from this area?" asked Torie.

"Well, most shifters were born and raised here," said Taylor.

"But, like you, most of us witches migrated here from somewhere else," added Jasmin. "Me, I'm from Oregon. I've only been here a couple of years, but I can't imagine living anywhere else."

"You came here after finding out you were a…witch?" Torie hesitated, then whispered the last word.

Jasmin laughed. "Girl, you don't have to act like you're saying something nasty. Yes, I was drawn here after discovering who I truly am."

"I find it fascinating that this happens to us as we get older," said Torie. "Why did I have to wait until now for this to happen?"

"Are you kidding?" said Jasmin. "Shit, if I had the kind of powers I have now in my twenties…I would probably be dead by now. What would we have done back then? Used our powers to make the high school mean girl's hair fall out? Given the cheerleaders boobs so big they couldn't pick them up off the ground?"

The images she created made Torie laugh out loud. "I would

probably have made Bobby Johnson grow inches of hair from every opening in his body and given him warts." She laughed uncontrollably. "He was the kid in Junior High that told everyone I gave him a hand job when I wouldn't let him kiss me under the bleachers one day. After that, I was known as Butter Churn for the entire next year."

The women roared in laughter. But then, slowly, as if remembering that there was a dark pall over their heads, the laughter stopped.

"I feel guilty," said Taylor, "having fun here, laughing. All while Eddie is near death, and so many of our brethren have been slaughtered."

Torie hung her head, feeling bad for bringing mirth to the group.

"Oh no, don't feel bad," said Taylor. "It was kind of nice to laugh again."

"So, I hate to ask, but does anyone have any leads on who is doing this to your community?" said Torie.

"Who," said Jasmin, "or what. Most of the shifters are peaceful creatures, living in harmony with one another. But they are still supernatural creatures, and therefore, should not be easy marks for whatever is hunting them."

"Unless it's another supernatural," said Fionna, looking around worriedly. "There are rumors that—" she stopped mid-sentence, her body stiffening and her head lifted, turning slightly in the way of the front door as it swung open.

"What is it?" said Torie, her eyes locking on the two men that walked into the shop.

Taylor frowned, staring at them as she whispered a single word. "Wolves."

# 8

"Wolves?" Torie said. "As in wolf shifters?"

Fionna leaned in close, her voice low and even. "Yes. But more."

Torie noticed the immediate tension in the room as the two men entered. They were both tall, lean of build with dark hair and eyes. One had a full beard while the other was clean shaven. They carried themselves with an air of authority, like they were not used to being questioned. She watched as they surveyed the room, one of them slightly tilting his head back a couple of times as he sniffed the air. He turned and looked at the group of women, nodding ever so slightly, and then made his way to the checkout counter.

"What do you feel?" whispered Jasmin.

Torie wasn't sure what she meant, but then as she watched the two men, she could feel a tingle in the pit of her stomach. It wasn't as if she had not encountered men like these before; they reminded her of the politicians and stock traders that Ward had often had to dinner at their home.

Cocky. Headstrong. Alpha.

But the way she felt when she looked at these two was completely different. She was on the verge of being physically ill the more she looked at them.

"They make me nauseous," she said.

Jasmin nodded. "They are more than just wolf shifters. Always trust your feelings around these types."

"What...what are they then?" Torie said, turning to Jasmin.

Before the witch could answer, she sat back in her chair, signaling for Torie to remain quiet. Torie turned just as the two men walked up to them.

"Hello, ladies," said the bearded one. "Taylor." He nodded in her direction; his eyes fixed on her.

She curled one lip, working hard to contain herself. "Max," she acknowledged.

The tension was broken by the other man, who leaned closer. "Hi, Taylor, Fionna, Jasmin. How are you?"

He was careful not to look them directly in the eye for too long, unlike his friend who had yet to break contact with Taylor.

"It's going to be a gorgeous day out. Ya'll have plans?"

"Uh, not really," said Fionna, clearly nervous.

"Oh, we might decide to go for a stroll later on," said Jasmin, her tone hard and direct, "maybe patrol for a killer. Or two."

Torie saw Fionna suck in a breath and hold it. The darker man, Max, turned his gaze to Jasmin, squinting slightly in her direction. He opened his mouth to speak, but his friend cut him off.

"So, who's this? I don't think I know you," he said, looking at Torie.

"No," said Jasmine, "you don't."

Now it was Torie's turn to cut the tension as she stood and offered her hand. "My name's Torie. I'm new in town."

He smiled, reaching to take her hand in his. "Nice to meet you. I'm Elric."

"Alright, let's go," said Max, grabbing Elric by the collar of his shirt. "I'm sure they have better things to do than listen to you." He turned as he was pulling the other man away. "Be seeing you, Taylor."

And with that, they were both out the door, leaving everyone in the bakery to breathe easier.

"What just happened?" asked Torie.

Fionna and Taylor exchanged glances and finally Fionna leaned in, still not willing to speak at normal volume.

"Do you remember what we were just saying about the theory that the person killing the shifters is a supernatural? Well, the victims have all been fairly small shifters. And those—" she nodded at the closed door, "are very big, very mean shifters."

"To be fair, we shouldn't paint them all with the same brush," said Taylor. "But the reports have all said that the victims were cut with something very sharp. And poisonous."

"And?" said Torie.

"Wolves have claws that can cut through anything," said Fionna. "And their bite carries a poison that is unique to them. It paralyzes their victims to prevent them from struggling."

Torie felt a cold sweat creep up her spine. She swallowed, her throat suddenly very dry.

"Here you go, ladies," said the baker. He had appeared out of the blue with a tray of muffins and coffees. All of them jumped at his approach. "I'm sorry. Shouldn't have sneaked up like that." He eyed the door as well before turning back to them. "Enjoy. Let me know if you need something else."

Torie eyed him as he walked back to the other side of the counter. She didn't miss the fact that he kept looking at the door, almost like he wanted to make sure there would be no more surprises walking in.

"I thought everyone in town was all peace and love," said Torie.

"For the most part we are," replied Jasmin. "But the wolves, they aren't from around here. They, and some of the other more extreme supernaturals, started drifting up from Trinity. They are still finding their place, if you will."

"So, what's up with this Trinity place?" asked Torie, reaching for a muffin and sinking her teeth into it. She heard herself actually 'umm' out loud at the first bite. Whatever this was, it was perfection. "I'm sorry, but this is the best muffin I have ever tasted. What is it?"

"It's made from elderberries and apples," said Fionna. "Jim is the best baker in state. He's a wood elf so he knows how to put all kinds of things together into amazing tasting treats."

Torie smiled, not sure what a wood elf was but anyone that could make something this delicious was okay in her book.

"Anyway, as far as Trinity Cove goes, it's another little town about an hour south of us," said Jasmin. "It's like Singing Falls, and completely different at the same time. It was overrun by darkness, literally, and is now a refuge for supernaturals like us, but ones that prefer the cover of darkness."

"Like the wolves," said Fionna. "Only lately they have been finding their way up here more and more. Not sure why, but here they are. For the most part, they leave us alone and we leave them alone."

"When did they start showing up?" asked Torie.

"About four months ago," said Jasmin, "around the same time the killings started." Her gaze grew hard, and Torie felt the tension start to build again.

"So, was I reading into things or was there something between the two of you?" Torie said, looking at Taylor.

She looked down, sipping the coffee in her hands. "Not at all. I own a small bookstore just off main here, and he walked in one day; said he followed my scent. Yeah, not creepy at all. He started with the whole 'made for each other' nonsense. He proceeded to get a little handsy; I wasn't having it. He wasn't used to not having his way. Hasn't really been cool with me since."

"Alpha level shifters can be real assholes," said Fionna. "Bears, lions, tigers...but wolves are the worst. For the most part they all stay down in Trinity. But every now and then, one seeks new hunting grounds."

"So what do you do about it?" said Torie. "I mean, if the majority of citizens in Singing Falls are supernaturals, why don't you get together and just run them out of town?"

"Yeah, cause a wolf shifter is really going to be terrified of a squirrel and a few bunnies," said Fionna, laughing.

Jasmin wasn't laughing, however. She glanced at Torie and smiled.

"I like the way you think," she said. "We need more witches like you in the community. But first, I take it you need to get a little more used to your powers. Learn just what being a witch is all about."

Torie nodded. Was this the person her mother had wanted her to learn from? Her mother was right about the town. She felt like this was where she belonged. Something occurred to her and she felt like she had to get it out.

"Hey, I can't help but notice, are all of you single? I mean, not you, Fionna, but are you two married?"

"Nope, single and free here," said Taylor.

"Witches don't do well with husbands," said Jasmin. "I was married, but to an ass. Of course, I couldn't see that he was an ass at first. But once I went through the change, it was like a veil lifted; he was ass all up and through."

Torie roared with laughter. "Trust me, I know what you mean. Let me guess, did he run off with his business partner too?"

Jasmin placed a hand on her hip. "First, he would have had to get off the couch to start a business to then have a partner to run off with. Second, she was a bar waitress he met while hanging out with his 'boys'. She was the neighborhood man-stealer...and he fell for her dirty ass."

"Okay, we don't slut shame," said Taylor, "remember, she wasn't the married one. Why should we be mad at her because she got around?"

"I'm not mad at her, I'm mad at him. Who knows what he could have brought home to me? That girl treated STDs like they were Pokémon; gotta catch 'em all."

Again, they laughed at the visual Jasmin had created.

"Did you want to get back at them?" asked Torie, taking the conversation in a more serious direction.

"Yeah, I wanted to. Considered all kinds of nasty little revenge spells that I wanted to cast on him. But in the end, I realized it wasn't worth it to give him my energy like that. Everything happens for a reason. Besides, if he hadn't cheated on me, I would never have ended up here." She reached over and took the hands of her two friends. "And that means I wouldn't have met these lovely women. So I let all that go and I'm better off for it."

Torie hoped that she would attain this level of forgiveness. Maybe one day; but not just yet. First things first,. She felt like she was a part of this new community after only a day. That kind of connection for her was rare; practically unheard of. If she were going to be here for any amount of time, she needed to help keep it safe.

That meant taking part in finding out who was preying on the people of this little town.

"So, what can I do?" she asked.

Fionna smiled. "Just be an ally. We don't need any more enemies."

"Oh, I can do that. As long as I can have another one of these elderberry muffins before we head back to the house."

"The best thing about living here is you get to go shopping for a new wardrobe after the first month," joked Taylor.

Torie frowned. "Okay, so I can understand not wanting to use witchcraft against our exes, but what about on ourselves? Isn't there a spell that we can cast that lets us eat all the carbs and sugars we want without gaining weight?"

Jasmin laughed heartily at this. "Oh, I like this one."

They spent a bit more time together before Taylor announced that it was time for her to go open her book store, which Torie promised to visit the next time she ventured into town, and Jasmin announced that she had to get going as well. She owned a holistic wellness shop specializing in herbs and potions designed to align ones inner and outer selves.

After they left, Torie thanked Fionna for introducing her to such strong, witty, women. It was a relief to talk to someone that didn't start the conversation with 'where do you summer?', or by announcing what charities they were on the board of.

She loved everything about Singing Falls.

As they walked out of the shop, Fionna linked arms with her and happily introduced her to everyone they passed on the walk back to the car. She also told Torie what everyone was if they were on the supernatural spectrum. Torie had never known that fairies, elves, wiccans—not the same as witches she learned—and shifters of all kinds, even existed. Let alone that they all lived in a tiny, bucolic town nestled in the mountains of North Carolina.

Everywhere she turned, a new world opened up to her.

The ride back to her mother's house was completed in silence as she reveled in the fresh mountain air, her senses opening in a way she had never imagined.

They pulled into the drive and she turned to Fionna. "Do you want to come in? I'm sure there is a pot of tea on the stove as we speak. It's not like I need another muffin, but I'd love to split one of these carrot ones with you if—"

Fionna's change in body language cut her off. She looked around, her eyes shifting in all directions, her nose quivering.

"Fionna? What is it? What's wrong?"

But rather than answer, Fionna was out of the car and sprinting toward the house. Torie followed her, her heart racing in fear.

The door was open just a crack and the two of them raced inside.

The house appeared to be in order, but Torie felt an uneasiness in the pit of her stomach. As she stepped farther inside, Fionna walked in front of her, holding out a hand to stop her.

"Torie, don't. Stay here; please."

"No way. Mom!" she called, "where are you?"

They made their way into the kitchen, and that was where the orderliness stopped. The room was a mess; plates were shattered, cabinet doors hung open, some off their hinges, and there were kitchen knives stuck in the wall.

"Mom!" screamed Torie, rushing past her friend to the workroom.

Her mother was there, lying face down on the large table, blood pooled around her, her head turned to one side, eyes glassy and staring.

"No!" screamed Torie. She turned and buried her face in Fionna's shoulder, holding onto her new friend for dear life, her mind refusing to accept the horror that had taken place in her mother's house.

## 9

"Mom? Mom, can you hear me?"

Torie felt a light touch on her shoulder, gently rousing her from a drug-induced stupor. She turned over, confusion clouding her eyes. A fog that threatened to keep her eyes closed weighed heavily on her. The face that was leaning over her was familiar, and warmth spread throughout her being as she recognized him.

"Shawn?" She tried to sit up, but he lightly placed a hand on her shoulder, urging her to remain lying back in bed. "What...what are you doing here? What time is it?"

"Easy, Mom." He smiled at her, his soft brown eyes bloodshot and puffy. He'd been crying. Who had made her beautiful child cry? "It's late; just after seven. Miss Freya had my number and called me."

"Freya called you? I told her not to do that. You have class and—"

"Mom, don't make me curse, but, well, eff those classes. No way I'm not being at your side at a time like this."

"Watch your mouth, young man. You know I hate it when you even hint at saying that word."

He smiled. Even now, she was thinking about him, and that made Shawn's guilt come flooding to the surface.

"Mom, I'm so sorry I didn't pick up when you called. I was so wrapped up in me; I should have answered." His tears started to flow again, but she quickly reached up and placed a finger on his lips.

"Don't. I knew you were in the midst of exams. I didn't want to bother you. I wanted to tell you about..." she hesitated, a lot of memories came flooding back to her. "Ward? Is he...I don't suppose he came?"

She saw her only child's visage change; he grew harder, his eyes cold. Guess someone had told him what happened.

"Haven't heard from him," Shawn said. "And honestly, it's probably a good thing he's not here." He turned away so that his mother couldn't see the hatred flooding his features.

"I'm sorry, Shawn, I don't know what to say."

He turned to face her, tears again burning streaks down his face. "Why are you apologizing for him? You always did that; and he always let you."

Had she? That was a trait she was unaware of, but once Shawn pointed it out, she knew it was true. Now it was her turn to look away.

Shawn reached out and took his mother's hand. "Look, anyone who would do what he has done...well, you're better off without him. But I don't really want to talk about him right now. I came because I wanted to be with you. I heard that you found Gram...is that true?"

Oh God...her mother. It all came rushing back to her, powering through the numbness the Ativan had brought on. Thank goodness Freya always had her travel-sized pharmacy with her.

The memories were bright and painful now. Her mother, face down in a pool of blood.

And she wasn't the only victim either. The body of the veterinarian, Ellie, was found outside in the woods adjacent to her mother's house. She had long gashes opened in her legs and torso. Later, the medical examiners would find long slivers of wood under her nails where she had clawed at tree trunks in a desperate attempt to escape whatever had dragged her into the forest.

Torie was sickened by what had happened to Ellie, but part of her was thankful her mother had been spared such a horrendous fate. Whatever killed her had not left a visible mark. At least not on the outside. But the fact that she had lost so much blood, from her mouth, her eyes and her ears, meant something had assaulted her from the inside.

The police had come and cordoned off the house. Fionna had called Glen, and together they had taken Torie back to their house. She was clearly in shock and managed to give them Freya's number when they kept insisting that she needed to see a doctor. Her friend had arrived within minutes. Or maybe it was days. Torie sat on the couch in her friends' living room with no connection to how much time may have passed. She was staring straight ahead, her gaze fixed and unwavering, until she noticed a hand moving up and down in front of her face.

She blinked, looking to one side and saw Freya's face come into focus. That was when she cried; great, devastating sobs that came from the depths of her soul and wrecked her body. This was a pain she never thought she could feel. Loss and sorrow collided in her, twisting her until she felt like someone had removed her heart and showed it to her just before they crushed it.

Freya held her, letting her cry as hard and as long as she needed. There came a point when Torie couldn't cry anymore; tears refused to come, but that didn't mean the pain stopped. *This had to be what it would feel like to lose one's child,* she thought. No, that wasn't true. If anything ever happened to Shawn, she would not be able to go on. That was a pain there would be no coming back from.

She let her friend rock her softly, whispering in her ear to get it out. Her head ached, her chest felt like it was on fire, and when she finally pulled back from Freya, her eyes were so dry that her vision blurred. She looked over at Fionna and Glen and saw that they too had been crying along with her.

That was when Freya had suggested something to help her sleep for a while and she gladly accepted.

That had been hours ago. Now she was face to face with her son and the memory that her mother was dead.

"Do they know what happened?" Torie asked.

Shawn shook his head. "It's going to be awhile before they get the autopsy report. They sent Gram's body to some hospital south of here to perform the autopsy."

She nodded. "Um, my friends, Fionna and Glen. Are they around?"

"We're right here," came Fionna's voice from just outside the guest room where Torie had been sleeping. She stepped slowly into the room. "Are you okay, Torie?" She seemed to catch herself and answer her own question. "Of course you're not okay...what kind of stupid question was that to ask?"

Her self-berating was almost enough to make Torie smile. She reached out and grasped her friend's hand, pulling her closer to the bed.

"Thank you," Torie said, "for bringing my son to me. I feel foolish, lying here like this."

"Nonsense," said Fionna. "I've already spoken to Glen; you're staying here for as long as you need. So no talk about being foolish."

"I...don't know what to say," Torie said. Part of her thought she should return to New York; but where would she stay? She couldn't afford an apartment, and while there was Freya...she knew that couldn't be a long-term solution. Besides, the thought of leaving Singing Falls threatened to make her heart break for a second time. She just nodded, swallowing back tears and patted Fionna's hand.

"Of course, you are welcome too, Shawn," she added, turning to the young man. "Your mother can probably use all the support she can get right now."

Torie frowned, looking from one to the other. How would she explain everything she had learned about this town to her son?

And did she even want to?

There was a killer on the loose here; one that was capable of killing supernaturals and witches. The last place she wanted her only child was Singing Falls.

"No, Shawn, that won't be necessary. I want you back at school—" she almost let the word 'safe' slip in but caught herself just in time. She glanced at Fionna, silently pleading with her friend.

"I mean, at least until the funeral is over," added Fionna. "After that, we'll see how you're doing."

Shawn smiled and stood up, stretching. "Well, I only have a couple more exams to take before I'm done with the semester. After that I'm coming back."

"But your trip—" started Torie.

"Is not as important as you are. Do you plan to go back to New York?"

"No. There is nothing there for me. I like it here. And I need to find out what happened to your Gram."

"Okay. Then I will definitely be returning after finals. I don't like you being alone up here in these mountains."

"She's not," came a voice from behind them. Glen walked in and sat on the side of the bed, smiling at Torie. "She will have more caregivers than you can imagine."

"Shawn, can you check on Freya for me?" Torie asked. "Let her know I'm feeling a little better."

"Sure," he answered, making his way out of the bedroom.

Once she was sure he was out of earshot, she whispered to her friends, "I don't want him up here. Please, I can't be sure he is safe; and how do I explain this town to him?"

Fionna nodded. "You're right. We will keep an eye on him until the funeral and then see him off. He deserves to say goodbye to his grandmother."

"Of course he does," said Torie. He was so different from his father. Ward could be charming, but disingenuous. But Shawn wore his feelings on his sleeve. He was sensitive and had always been in touch with his feelings. He was his mother's child, and the fact that she was hurting made him hurt. It wouldn't be easy getting him to leave.

"So, do either of you know what happened?" Torie asked. She watched the two of them exchange quick glances, their faces masks of worry. "It's okay, I promise. I can take whatever you need to tell me. Oh...I just thought of something; what about Eddie?"

"He wasn't there," said Glen. "We don't know what happened to him. I did ask around at the hospital...they sent your mom's body down to Trinity. From a preliminary standpoint, they are pretty sure it's poison, but they can't identify what or how it was administered."

"What about Ellie?" Torie asked.

"She was killed by..." Glen paused, collecting herself. "She was killed by blunt force trauma and exsanguination. She bled out, basically."

"It's so weird," said Fionna, "I was the one who found her body. I could smell blood that didn't belong to your mother and followed the scent outside."

Torie nodded; she remembered Fionna telling her to stay there and not move before she ran out the back door, across the patio and up into the line of trees that formed just beyond the property marker of her mother's house.

"I found Ellie lying there, sliced nearly to ribbons. But the strange thing was, there was no other supernatural scent around her."

"Wolves," said Glen, her face growing hard. "I mean it had to be."

"But I would have smelled them," said Fionna.

"Not necessarily," said Glen. "I've been researching the wolves that came up from Trinity. Unlike other shifters, they can take on hybrid forms...half wolf, half man."

"What?" said Torie, "you mean like werewolves?"

"Exactly. They are capable of hiding their true nature, even to other supernaturals."

"Christ. All the more reason I don't want Shawn staying here," Torie replied.

"If they are the ones responsible for this, what motive do they have?" Fionna asked.

Glen looked at her in consternation. "Why do they need a motive? You know, maybe it's hunger, pure and simple. They are predators, and they stumble upon a community of peace-loving shifters that are no match for them physically. Maybe they think they stumbled on an all you can eat buffet. And that," she took her lover's face in her hands, "is why I don't want you wandering around alone until this is all over."

Torie choked back tears. Their love was so pure, and the depth of it made her realize it was something she and Ward had never shared; no matter how she had tried to convince herself otherwise.

"But why my mother?" she asked.

Both were silent at that. Finally, Glen spoke up, her voice cracking.

"No idea. Your mother was beloved by everyone in the community. No one had a harsh word to say about her. She was kind and giving...she would literally give you the food off her plate if you asked for it."

Tears streamed down the woman's face as Fionna wrapped an arm around her, comforting her. "Maybe it was her vision."

"What vision?" asked Torie.

"Well, witches have different gifts, aside from their ability to work magics. They have the skills they are born with; the ones that manifest naturally as part of their being. One of your mother's was the gift of sight. She could foresee things. Maybe the killer knew that and was afraid he couldn't hide from that."

Glen nodded. "I hadn't thought of that. It's possible. Like they were eliminating a threat before it presented."

"You mean my mother could see the future?"

"Yes," said Fionna. "But she would never speak about what she saw."

Torie began to fret. "Do you think...do you think she foresaw this?"

Glen's eyes grew misty and she looked away, unable to hold Torie's gaze.

"I think, this explains why she was so insistent on you going out the morning it happened."

Torie felt her heart leap into her throat. Her mother had given her life to protect her. There was no way in hell she was letting this go unavenged.

"Where do we start?" Torie said.

Fionna nodded. "I say we have a heart to heart with a couple of wolves who have been prowling around town. And I know just where to find them."

## 10

"We can't just go waltzing up to a wolf and interrogate him," said Jasmin.

Fionna and Glen had called her to come over for a strategy session. As soon as she arrived, she threw her arms around Torie.

"Your mother was a great woman," she said into her ear. "She will not be forgotten. And we are going to get the bastard doing this."

Torie broke her grip and thanked her for the sentiment. She took a moment to walk into the living room, checking on Shawn. He was immersed in a texting conversation with friends from school and didn't notice when she increased the volume on the television slightly before easing back into the kitchen.

"So why can't we just ask them what they've been up to? For that matter, why don't we ask them once and for all what they are doing here in town?"

"Because they are wolves," said Jasmin. "They are all instinct and action. No reflection at all. If they sense they are being accused of something, or backed into a corner, they might come out swinging."

"Then what would you suggest?" said Torie.

"This will be hard," said Jasmin, "but I've called Taylor and asked her to meet us at your mother's house. I'm going to cast a spell to see if I can uncover any trace of the supernatural in the vicinity where she was killed. And I want Taylor to go over every inch of the woods. As sensitive as Fionna's nose might be, Taylor is a fox shifter. There is nothing she can't track. Between us, if it's there, we will find it."

"And if it *is* a wolf?" said Fionna. "What do we do next?"

"We call the authorities and have them arrested, right?" said Torie.

They all looked at her, bewildered.

"There is no jail for supernaturals," said Glen. "Supernaturals deal with their own." The finality of her words told Torie what exactly she meant by that.

"And that leads to another question," said Fionna. "Let's say we do prove that this is the work of wolves. How do we bring them to justice? I mean, I don't think there are any shifters in town strong enough to take *one* down; let alone two of them."

Silence permeated the kitchen as they all considered what to do.

"We could try to find a hunter," said Glen.

"What's a hunter?" asked Torie.

"There are certain humans, born with the ability to fight and hunt supernaturals. It's the universe's way of keeping balance. There are many names for them; hunters, chosen ones, night stalkers...you name it. I think there is someone in Trinity that knows someone who could find us one."

Jasmine rolled her eyes. "I hate the thought of bringing one of them here. All that attitude, the tight leather pants, strutting around like they are God's gift. They are children with more brawn than brains."

"They do get the job done, however," said Taylor.

"The problem with hunters is that where they go, chaos follows," said Jasmin. "It's like they feed on it or something. And they will wear you out with all the moaning and complaining and 'woe is me' nonsense. I feel like just shaking one. I mean, they have it all; they're young, strong, usually gifted with magic for no reason, and spend a lot of time pouting over some random guy who usually turns out to be an ass but for some reason, is obsessed with the one hunter...don't get me started."

The other's looked at her in silence before bursting out laughing. "Well, as long as you don't get started on them," said Glen through her laughter.

"You know, I knew one once," said Fionna. "She was just like that. And really, I don't know how she survived in the summer. All that leather everywhere. And those hideous boots she would wear!"

"Ugh, don't get me started on those," said Jasmin, "and let me guess; she carried a ridiculous knife?"

"Knives everywhere! Plus a sword and all kinds of throwy things."

"They do like blades," said Jasmin. "I often wonder what would happen to one of them if she tripped and fell down a hill. Would she be stabbed repeatedly about her entire body from all the weapons hidden in her clothes?"

Even Torie had to laugh at that. "It kind of makes me want to meet one."

"Well, even if we could find one, who knows how long it would take to get here. We don't have that long. Whoever is doing this has struck and killed twice in two days," said Jasmin.

"You're assuming that Eddie is..." started Fionna.

"Possibly. The fact that he is missing now is not a good sign."

"Torie," said Jasmin, "are you sure you're up to this? Going back to your mother's house I mean."

She nodded. At some point she had to walk back through that door again. At least this way she would feel like it wasn't just to mourn.

"Is it okay if Shawn stays here?" she asked Fionna and Glen.

"Of course," was the reply. "There is plenty of junk food in the pantry. Hopefully we won't be out too long."

They paraded through the living room where Torie told her son she was running out with her friends. Freya eyed them suspiciously, and Torie promised her she would explain later, but for right now could she just keep an eye on Shawn.

Torie knew her oldest friend was sensing something was amiss...

Torie had never kept her out of the loop like this before, but she agreed. She was there to support her friend in whatever way was needed.

They piled into two cars and made the drive back to Alva's house. As one, they made their way to the front porch and stood there, giving Torie as much time as she needed.

Taking a deep breath, Torie pushed the door open and stepped across the threshold.

"Shouldn't there be…I don't know, detectives or police crawling all over the place?" she asked.

Fionna shook her head. "No. The sheriff handling this is actually a dwarf. He's one of us and is working with us on this. Things are handled very differently here."

Torie was starting to see just how different the town was as she made her way into the house. There was a rustling noise that came from the back, through the kitchen and near the workroom. Torie and her friends all jumped and huddled together, clinging onto one another for dear life.

That was when Taylor stepped into view, walking out of the kitchen with a bag of chips in one hand. "Hello, ladies, what's up? Why do you all look like that; like you've seen a ghost?" She turned and looked behind her.

"You scared us half to death," said Jasmin, shaking herself free of the others. "And why y'all up on me like this?"

"Well, I thought you, being the witch, would be the one to protect us. You know, throw a fireball or something," said Torie.

"A fireball?" said Jasmin, incredulously. "Who throws fireballs? What kind of shit have you been reading? Because whatever it is, I am not that kind of witch." She straightened her dress and they continued into the kitchen.

"Hey, Torie, I am so sorry about your mama," Taylor said, hugging her close. "What can I do to help?"

"Well, did you pick up on anything in here?" asked Fionna.

Taylor shook her head. "Nothing out of the ordinary. It's weird. The workroom smells almost too clean; like it's been disinfected."

"Did your mother clean before you arrived, or since you've been here?" asked Jasmin.

Torie shrugged. "I don't know. I mean, I told her I was coming so she may have."

"No," said Taylor, "this is recent. The crime scene has been cleaned."

"Maybe by the killer," said Fionna. "Maybe they cleaned it right after—" She stopped herself, not wanting to finish that sentence. "That would explain why I didn't smell anything at all when we found her."

"Have you been out back yet?" asked Jasmin. "To the site where they found Ellie?"

"No, I was waiting for you guys to get here. You know I'm not fond of the woods," Taylor said.

Jasmin rolled her eyes. "Who ever heard of a fox afraid of the woods?"

She didn't wait for an answer, and instead, placed a large bag with a rope tie that was cinched closed onto the center island in the kitchen.

"What's that?" asked Torie.

"My tools of the trade," Jasmin replied. She opened the bag and began removing the contents and placing them one by one on the granite island. A jar with a cork stopper in place. Two large feathers, one white the other black; several crystals that she then scattered about the island; a long wooden root, and a large crystal ball that she then placed in the midst of all the other items.

"Nice crystal ball," said Torie, immediately drawn to it.

"Thanks," she replied. "We'll get you one soon. Every witch should have her own. Just be careful with it. Don't leave it lying around the house without a cloth covering it."

"Oh. Because of the spirits it might call?" asked Fionna, gazing over Jasmin's shoulder.

"What? No, not because of spirits. Because it will reflect any sunlight streaming through the windows and burn your house down."

"Oh," said Fionna, almost sounding disappointed. She preferred the thought of spirits rather than plain old combustion via carelessness.

"So, what are you going to do?" Torie said, "and can I help?"

"You know, you just might be able to." She picked up the two feathers and handed them to Torie. "The blood bond between witches is powerful, it is almost impossible to break. I may be able to use you to help anchor the emotions in this house, to clear away all the negativity created by an unnatural death, to help see what really happened here."

She gave the feathers to Torie and told her to stand in the center of the kitchen. "No matter what you see or hear…or think you're hearing, do not let go of these feathers," she said.

She asked Glen and the shifters to step aside, and then she lifted one of the blue crystals she had cast over the island, turning it over and over in her hand. She picked up the wooden root in her other hand and closed her eyes. Holding the crystal aloft, she began to chant, her voice low and powerful as she called upon ancient spirits to aide her.

*"Oh lady of the evening and servant of the night,*
*show us what was done in dark can be brought to light.*
*I beseech your wisdom, so great and vast,*
*to show me now, the images of the past."*

With that, she cast the crystal onto the floor, along with the wooden root. Then, she picked up the jar, undid the stopper and poured a gray powder into her hand. With great reverence, she bowed to the powder, and then cast it into the air, spreading it into an arch around the kitchen.

The powder hung in place, not sinking or spreading out; rather it stayed where she threw it and then began to glow blue. Slowly, it stretched outward, settling in place as it sought to recreate what had just happened only hours before in the space.

Torie heard a low moan in the air, it came from everywhere and nowhere at the same time, and it reverberated in her being, like the vibrations of a song filled with bass when played too long. She could feel the vibrations in her teeth.

The powder created an image in the center of the room. It was vague at first, but slowly it coalesced into the ghostly form of a figure.

It was her mother, and Torie gasped at the sight.

Alva was cleaning the kitchen, placing the empty whiskey bottle into the recycling bin and then the tumblers into the sink. Suddenly, she turned and faced someone who was outside of the field of view of the powder.

Her lips moved silently as she spoke with someone. To Torie, it was like watching an old silent film from the twenties. There was movement, but no sound.

She watched as the transparent form of her mother stiffened and then waved her arm before her, casting a wave of power that disrupted the vision the powder was creating. Everything wavered, disappearing in the way Torie envisioned a desert mirage would.

"No! What happened?" Torie asked.

"Your mother activated a pre-set spell. One that was meant to block the kind of viewing I just attempted," said Jasmin. "Whatever happened to her, she didn't want us seeing it."

"Why? Why would she do that?" said Torie, her voice raw with emotion.

"Why, to protect you of course."

They turned just in time to see the visage of Alva shimmer into view before them.

"Oh, come now. You ladies act like you've never seen a ghost before."

## 11

"Mom?" said Torie, staring at the apparition. "Is that really you? How are you here?"

"Oh, my time on this plane isn't over just yet."

Jasmin moved quickly, placing herself between the ghostly figure and the other women. "Stand back. This could be a trick." She reached out and picked up one of the crystals, holding it in her fist menacingly.

"Jasmin, really? A conjuring stone...what, are you going to reverse the spell and use it to entrap me? I taught you that spell, remember? Do you really think I don't know how to counter it?"

"If you are truly Alva, tell us something that only she would know," said Jasmin.

"Alright." The ghost turned to address the group of friends. "Ladies, do you remember a couple of years ago when Jasmin caught that mysterious flu and was out of commission for three days? She was so sick that none of us were allowed to visit her for fear she would infect us? Well, in truth, she had tried to create her own version of female Viagra via magics; and it caused her to grow a—"

"That's enough," interrupted Jasmin. "It is truly you." She dropped her guard and the crystal she was holding.

"Wait, let her finish," said Taylor. "What did you grow?" The others looked at her, their combined sigh telling her to figure it out for herself. "Oh...Oh! Wow...what did you do with it?"

"Taylor, not now," said Fionna, turning to the ghostly witch floating in the center of the room. "Alva...why are you still here? And don't say your time isn't up. That's not how ghostly incarnation works."

"I don't think I was supposed to die just yet. I can't cross over. I feel trapped."

"It's because a great injustice happened here," said Jasmin. "I've heard about this before. Witches can be tied to the place of their death if that death was one of great violence or...was an accident. If it happens before the witch's time, then the other side was not prepared to receive her."

Torie stepped forward slowly. She reached out, her hand passing through her mother's form as easily as it would smoke from a blown-out candle.

"Oh, my daughter," said Alva, reaching out to lay an ephemeral palm against her daughter's cheek. "I think I held on because, as my body lay dying, I thought of you and how my only regret was that we were only just getting reacquainted...and I needed more time with you."

"Great longing and sadness," said Jasmin. "Yes, that could do it. That would have anchored you to this world."

"How long are you here for?" asked Torie. Part of her mind was telling her that she should be freaking out; but after everything else she had seen, this was just one more weird occurrence to add to the list of weird occurrences she was experiencing. None of that mattered to her now; her mother was standing—or rather floating—before her now. And that was enough.

"I've no idea. I wasn't sure I would ever find my way back. I didn't think it was possible to come back like this. I mean, sure, ghosts are real; but no one really knows how they are created. No matter how smart they think they are." She gave Jasmin a knowing stare and then an infectious smile.

"What was it like, Alva?" said Jasmin.

"Being dead? It sucked. It was scary as all get out. I mean, one minute I knew I was alive, then it was like someone just flicked a switch and turned everything off. You know how there are times when you're so tired that you get into bed and suddenly it's the next morning, you wake up and you don't even remember falling asleep? It was like that. Only this right now is the next morning. I don't remember dreaming or anything. Just bits of aches and restlessness until suddenly I saw the light from your spell, and it was like an alarm clock. Only I woke up and realized I was dead...yet here I am."

Fionna started to cry and was quickly joined by Taylor.

"Hey, what is this? What's going on?" said Alva, floating over to stand next to her friends.

"It's just so sad," said Fionna. "I mean, you're...gone. I miss you so much." Taylor nodded furiously, echoing her friend's sentiments.

"Well, think of me not so much as being gone; just different."

"I feel like I just got you back," said Torie, "and now you're..." She choked up, feeling the tears begin to flow. "I never got to say goodbye to you."

"Well, we have time now. Maybe I'm here a day, a week...who knows. But we will have our time. There are still things we need to talk about."

"Like who did this to you," said Jasmin. "Can you tell us that?"

Alva looked perplexed. Her translucent features grew distant as she stared at the group of women.

"I...I don't know. Isn't that strange? I can remember everything up until the point just before the lights went out, but I don't know what happened or who did it."

"What exactly do you remember?" said Torie.

"I had just finished washing out the tumblers and had put on a kettle for tea. I thought I heard Eddie cry out, so I rushed into the workroom...and then...that's it. I don't remember anything beyond that."

"You obviously put up a fight, judging from the state of the kitchen," said Jasmin. "And you activated a spell that kept me from seeing what happened. Why would you cast a spell like that?"

Alva grew quiet, once again lost in contemplation. "I have no idea, Jasmin. It's like there's a big black spot in my memories. I don't know what happened. How is Eddie, is he okay?"

Jasmin took a deep breath. "He's missing, Alva."

"He was gone when we arrived," said Fionna.

"Oh," said Alva. "Wait, did you...did you find me? You and—" She turned in the air, facing Torie. "Oh, my baby..."

Torie began to cry again, the memories were too fresh, and she recoiled from them, blocking out the pain as much as possible.

"I'm so sorry you had to see me like that," she whispered.

"It was so awful," said Fionna. "Well, much more so for you and Ellie than for us, but—"

"Ellie? What do you mean for Ellie?"

Fionna stumbled over her words, the look of shock on her face told them she had not considered that Alva did not know.

"Alva, honey, do you remember Ellie coming over?" asked Jasmin.

Alva shook her head. "No. She was supposed to at some point to check in on Eddie and let us know what she found out from the lab in Trinity. But she hadn't arrived before...you know."

"Did she call you?"

"Sure. She said she had some surprising news from the blood sample she had taken from Eddie. But she never arrived. Why? What aren't you telling me?"

Jasmin swallowed hard. "Alva, Ellie was killed as well."

Then, just when Torie thought her heart could not possibly hurt any more, her mother, her dead mother, began to cry. It was a long, sorrowful wail that raised the hair on the back of her neck. She had never wanted to throw her arms around anyone more than she did at that moment.

"I'm sorry," said Fionna, stepping back, "I really just assumed you knew. That you were, I don't know, together in the afterlife."

Jasmin gave her a look that told her to stop speaking.

"So, wait," said Taylor, "if she wasn't here before you...passed, then maybe she walked in on whoever did it. Maybe that's what all of this—" she waved at the wreckage of the kitchen, "is from."

Jasmin nodded. "Could be. Ellie isn't a supernatural. She would have put up a fight if she surprised the killer. She was pretty spry, and she practiced judo as well."

"And all those Pilates classes would have come in handy too," said Fionna. "She was a lot stronger than she looked."

"Where was she?" said Alva, turning her attention back to the ladies.

"Outside," said Torie. "She was…in pretty bad shape."

"Yeah," said Jasmin, "like, wolf bad shape."

"That's why we asked Taylor to meet us here," said Fionna. "To see if she can sniff out something that I might have missed."

"A wolf," said Alva. "As in the two that have been prowling around town lately?"

"We don't know," said Torie. "But I promise you, I'm going to find out who did this to you, Mom."

"No, you're not, Torie," said Alva, turning to face Jasmin. "I forbid it, Jasmin. I wanted you to teach her, help bring her into her power; but I don't want her put in harm's way like this."

Torie was touched that even though her mortal shell had been lost, her mother still wanted to protect her, even from the beyond.

"I'm going to watch over her," said Jasmin, "don't you worry about that. But we have to stop this killer, Alva. You. Ellie. Eddie. Everyone else we've lost to this psychopath. I can't take it anymore. It has to end."

"But that's what we have the police for," said Taylor. "Let them do their job."

"Yeah, cos they've done it so well up to this point," said Jasmin. "No, this is supernatural crime. It's time we handled it our way."

"Are the police here not part of the community?" asked Torie.

"They are," replied Alva, "but they have a different code they have to follow."

Torie didn't say anything. She had never been a believer in vigilante justice, but she had also never been touched by crime in such a personal way.

"Torie, there isn't really anything I can do to stop you, but just think about this before you embark," said Alva. "You have a child now. Ward is out of the picture; if anything happens to you, Shawn will be all alone."

This hit Torie like the proverbial train. She felt like her chest had just caved in and there suddenly wasn't enough oxygen in the room to sustain her. She sat on the couch, her world spinning.

"That was a low blow," Jasmin said, frowning at her dead friend.

"I...I'm sorry," said Alva, slightly confused. "I don't know why I would have said something like that."

"Look, we aren't talking about taking on the wolves ourselves. *If* they did this," said Fionna. "We just need to get some proof that we can turn over to the authorities. Right?"

"Yeah. Right," said Jasmin.

"Fine. But I don't want you doing this just for me," said Alva. She floated near her daughter and again held a ghostly hand up to her head. "I have lived a long, happy life. I died in a place I loved, after having reconnected with the daughter I love. I am at peace with this."

"Thank you, Mom," said Torie. "But I agree with Jasmin...this isn't just to avenge you. It is to make this place safer for everyone who lives here." She forced a smile, as much for everyone in the room as it was for herself. Her mother's words about Shawn had already wormed their way deep into her mind and were beginning to haunt her.

"Taylor," said Fionna, looking at her friend. "What is it?"

Taylor's body was ramrod stiff and she was staring out the back of the house. Then, in the blink of an eye, she dropped her human form and became a fox. She hurried through the house and out the back sliding door that was open. She began sniffing around the patio and then launched full speed for the tree line behind the house.

The other's ran after her out the door. All except Alva. She stopped at the open slider, unable to exit.

"Mom, what is it?" Torie asked, turning to face her.

"I don't know. I can't leave," she replied. "Torie...I can't leave the house. I don't know how I know that, but I do. Go, see what Taylor has found."

Torie hesitated for a moment, but then made her way to the woods where she could see her friends. She was huffing when she got there. All those yoga and aerobics classes she had spent hours in and for what? Jumping around on an exercise mat was not the same thing as running up a grass hill.

"What...what is it?" she asked.

"There's a wolf prowling around out here," said Taylor after shifting back to her human form. "I saw him from the house, and then caught his scent. But by the time I got up here he was gone."

"He couldn't have just disappeared," said Jasmin.

"Oh, he didn't," came a voice from behind us. They turned, and deeper into the woods, a shape separated from the shadows of the trees, and Elric the werewolf stepped forward.

## 12

This time Jasmin did step forward, placing her body between the wolf and the other women.

"Easy there," said Elric, raising both hands, "I'm not here to hurt anyone."

"What are you doing skulking about up here?" asked Fionna.

"I heard about the death of the witch. I knew who she was." He gave Torie a sorrowful look. "I wanted to make sure you were okay, and maybe to pay my respects."

Torie flinched at his openness. He seemed genuinely upset at her loss; and that made her suspicious.

"You seem almost...guilty," Torie said. "Why would that be?"

"And where's your friend?" said Jasmin, looking around.

"Oh, he...he's not here. And he's not really my friend."

"Oh, bullshit on that. You're practically inseparable. As a matter of fact, I've never seen the two of you apart," Taylor said.

"He's my alpha...I don't have a choice," said Elric.

"What do you know about what's going on around here?" asked Torie.

"Only what I've heard from Max. He said something is hunting shifters in this area."

"And that doesn't scare you?" said Fionna.

Elric huffed. "Hardly. There's not much out there that can hurt a wolf." He gave Torie a nervous, sideways glance.

"Why do you keep looking at her?" asked Taylor.

"Her magic," said the wolf, "I can smell it on her." He then glanced at Jasmin. "Yours too. Like I said, there isn't much that can hurt us...except witches really."

That caught their attention. It was like being a child and learning that a night-light was all it took to keep away the boogey man.

"Why are you up here?" said Jasmin. "I hear that Trinity Cove is more your speed."

Elric shuffled his feet. "It was. But things got a little rough down there; even for us. There are some powerful witches running things in that town. And the biggest one of all isn't too keen on wolves; even though rumor has it she keeps one as a pet."

Jasmin looked at Torie, her eyes lighting up with an idea. "Elric, if we ask you something, will you answer us truthfully?"

He nodded, urging her to continue.

"Where were you and Max the morning Alva was killed?"

He took a step back, gray eyes narrowing. "You think we did this?"

"We don't know what to think," said Torie hastily. She took a step toward the wolf, showing him that she wasn't afraid. "But we need to find out who killed my mother and our friend."

"Well it wasn't us," he said. "You know, Max said at some point we would be blamed, but I promise you we had nothing to do with it."

Jasmin nodded. "He's telling the truth."

The certainty of her words made Elric flinch. "Did you just use magic on me?"

"A harmless revelation spell. It would have alerted me if you were lying."

"Wait, you can do that?" said Taylor. "And you never told us? Geez, that would have saved me from going on a lot of dates that ended badly."

"You shouldn't be dating at your age anyway," said Fionna, teasingly.

"Maybe not all of us are ready to settle down and pull the dirt over our bodies," she said. Immediately she realized just how much of her foot was in her mouth and gave an 'I'm sorry' look to Torie.

"One of these days I'm really going to buy you that muzzle," said Jasmin.

"It's okay," said Torie. The more time she spent with these women, the more she realized it was impossible to be upset with them. They had nothing but the best intentions for her, and coming from her previous life, that was something she truly appreciated. "But I'm not sure standing around out here is getting us anywhere."

They agreed and headed back to the house, Torie leading the way, Elric bringing up the rear.

"Where do you think you're going?" said Jasmin, turning to the wolf.

"I just thought maybe..." he stammered.

"It's okay, Jasmin," Torie said. "Let him come in." She stopped at the threshold, looking back at Elric. "So, do I have to invite you in or something?"

Jasmin rolled her eyes. "He's not a vampire, Torie."

"Yeah, and that doesn't work with them anyway," Elric said, "they can pretty much go wherever they want."

All the women turned to look at him with blank faces.

"Well, that's a pleasant thought," said Jasmin under her breath. "The more you know I guess."

"So, what now?" asked Taylor. "If a wolf isn't doing this, then we are pretty much back at square one."

"Well, maybe not," said Jasmin. "Maybe we are looking too far ahead. Trying to figure out who the killer is without having enough to go on."

"Go on," said Torie as she put on a kettle of water.

"Well, maybe we need to look at why the killer changed their M.O."

"M.O? What's that?" asked Taylor.

"Method of Operation," said Fionna. "What? I watch *Law and Order*...it's on every channel, you know."

"Yes," continued Jasmin. "Up until this point, the killer has exclusively gone after shifters, right?"

There was murmured agreement just as the kettle began to squee loudly. Torie took out multiple cups and a selection of teas. Each of the women picked out the ones they wanted and added it to their cup.

"What about you?" said Torie, glancing at Elric. "What kind would you like?"

He seemed confused and made his way to the island. "What is it?"

"It's tea," Torie said. "Have you never had it before?"

Elric shook his head, his slightly too long salt and pepper hair catching the light streaming through the windows.

"You look like an Earl Grey kind of guy," said Torie, plopping a bag into the cup and adding the water. "Give it a few minutes to steep then give it a sip." She turned back to Jasmin, motioning for her to continue.

"So, if the killer is only interested in shifters, why kill Alva? She's a witch. And then why kill Ellie? She was human."

"Well, maybe the killer did it to throw everyone off their trail?" offered Fionna.

"But that would mean that we were on their trail to begin with," said Jasmin, "and we weren't anywhere close to learning who they were."

"Maybe they knew something that scared them," said Elric as he slowly took his first sip of tea. His gray eyes lit up and he smiled as the warm elixir hit his throat. "Okay, this is awesome."

"What did you say?" said Jasmin.

"I said this is awesome."

"No, before that."

"Oh, maybe the killer changed his pattern to protect himself. You might not have been close, but maybe Torie's mom, or the other lady you mentioned, were."

No one said anything as they all regarded his words in silence.

"My mother said she doesn't remember anything," said Torie. "And as far as I know, Ellie isn't floating around here for us to ask her." She hesitated before turning to Jasmin. "Is she? Hanging around here I mean?"

Jasmin shrugged. "No idea. But that would be highly unlikely. She would have no personal attachment to this place; nothing to anchor her."

"What was it she was doing the night before?" asked Torie, snapping her fingers as she paced the kitchen to jog her memory.

"She was taking Eddie's lab samples to Trinity to get them analyzed," said Fionna. "She always thought we were dealing with some type of poison or something like that. She thought that was how the killer was incapacitating their victims."

"That's right," said Jasmin. Suddenly, Elric's hypothesis held a lot more weight. "If she found something, something that could be related to the killer, or gave her a clue…"

"Then she would be someone to take out," said Torie. "But why my mother? She didn't know anything."

"Maybe she wasn't the target," said Taylor. "Maybe she just happened to be here, and the killer somehow knew this was where Ellie would show up."

"Good thinking," said Jasmin.

"Really?" said Taylor, her features lifting at the compliment.

"Yes, really. See, this is why our collective brainpower is needed for this. Now, we need to figure out what Ellie could have known."

"Hey, I'm sorry, but…can I have some more?" said Elric. He had turned up his entire cup and drained it.

"Umm, sure," said Torie, "though you might want to take it easy at first." She laughed, happy that someone was enjoying this space where her mother had so recently passed away. The thought made her sad again, but then she remembered her mother wasn't completely gone. That would take a lot of getting used to, but it also made her wonder just where her mother was.

"Mom?" she called out, looking around. "Where are you?"

Elric stood as still as a board, his spine ramrod straight as he watched the women look about the house. What was happening here? Did they not realize that the old witch was gone?

"Hey, what are you doing?" he asked. "She's...you know, gone." He wasn't sure what to say. Maybe this was a human thing. Wolves did not mourn their dead, and they certainly didn't call out for them after the fact.

"She's a ghost now," said Taylor. Her matter-of-fact tone made the hair on the back of Elric's neck stand up. "You're looking like you see one now."

The wolf narrowed his eyes. "I have seen my fair share of ghosts, or haints, as the wolves call them, when I was in Trinity. They are strange, ephemeral creatures that floated about in the woods, wailing in longing, always searching it seemed, but no one knew what they were searching for. As a young pup they used to freak me out; and even now, as a full-grown shifter, I still shiver at the mention of them."

He joined the women in looking around at thin air, even though he had no idea what he was looking for.

"Is she...in the house?" he asked.

"Well of course she is," said Torie. "Where else would she be?"

Elric had no answer for that. Truthfully, he wasn't sure he wanted to know.

Torie started to panic. "What if she has moved on? She said she had no idea how long she was here. I mean, I barely got to see her as it was."

Before she could work herself into a full-blown panic, she heard the now familiar soft tones of her mother.

"What is all this carrying-on about?" she asked, materializing in front of Torie.

"Mom, I thought...I don't know what I thought. But you're still here."

"I am. For now, it seems."

"Alva," said Jasmin, "where were you?"

"I don't really know. You left the house, headed for the woods, and I knew I couldn't follow. Once you left the house and I was here alone, I just...went back."

"Back? To where?" Torie asked.

"I don't know. I just wasn't here anymore. Then I heard you calling for me and I...well, here I am." She turned around, taking notice of everyone around her, before locking eyes on Elric. "A wolf. As I live and breathe, a werewolf standing here in my own home."

Elric fought the urge to flee out the back door, forcing himself to take a step forward. He bowed at the ghost, nodding his head in deep respect. "Ma'am, I'm Elric, and it's nice to meet you."

Alva nodded in return. "And you as well." She turned her attention back to the women. "Well, what did you find up there?"

"Not much," said Taylor, "just this stray."

"But we might have a plan for our next step," said Jasmin. "Alva, I know that you don't remember who did this to you, but I need you to think hard about this. Did you tell anyone that Ellie was coming here to check on Eddie?"

Alva seemed to pause, the light of her ghostly form seeming to pulse slowly as she considered her old friend's words.

"I...I don't know. I think...maybe, but I don't know. I feel like I should know, but it's just not there."

"That's okay, Mom," said Torie. "Don't strain yourself." She was about to say something else when her phone buzzed. She took it out of her pocket and her face went ashen at the text she was reading.

"Torie," said Fionna, rushing to her side. "What is it? What's happened?"

"It...It's the coroner's office. They said they have the autopsy report back on..." She looked at her mother's form. "They said they want me to come to the medical examiner's office and they will give me the details, the death certificate and...and I can make arrangements for her funeral."

Despite the fact her mother was floating not two feet away from her, the news brought on not only her own tears, but somewhere, behind the ectoplasmic form she had become, her mother cried as well.

## 13

The funeral was a somber affair. It had taken Torie less time than she would have thought to do all the paperwork needed to close out her mother's death. Of course it helped that the cause of death printed on the paperwork had been listed as suicide.

Torie had been too shocked when she saw this to speak. She felt like someone had punched her in the stomach and driven the last vestiges of oxygen from her lungs. The world around her had slowed and dropped away when the coroner told her their findings. Jasmin and Fionna had immediately jumped on the Medical Examiner, yelling in tandem that he had lost his mind. They had known Alva for a decade and there was no way this woman would have taken her own life.

Torie didn't fight it. She didn't have the strength. During the chaos, everyone yelling at the coroner, all tears and rage, she simply reached across the desk, took the certificate, folded it and placed it in her purse. Then she got to her feet, holding the edge of the desk to steady her, and plodded slowly towards the door.

"Torie? Torie, where are you going?" It was Jasmin. They were in the same room, but she might as well have been yelling to her from another building. Everything receded from Torie's senses and all she wanted was to be out of this space that smelled like too much disinfectant and breathe some fresh air.

Once outside, she gulped in several lungfuls, then headed slowly for Jasmin's Subaru Outback and tried to open the locked door on the passenger's side. The fact that it would not open enraged her and she began to beat at the window with her purse, screaming at the door. She fell against it, trying to no avail to force the lock open. Slowly, she slid down the car until she was a heap on the asphalt, sobbing uncontrollably.

The hand on her shoulder was like an emotional balm, helping to reduce the sting of emotions that had been rubbed raw lately.

"Torie, it's okay. We are going to get this worked out," said Fionna, dropping to her knees to hug her friend.

"I...I don't want it worked out," said Torie. "What I want is to get the bastard who did this to my mother."

"We will. I promise you we will."

"But let's get you home first," said Jasmin, her voice full of concern.

Torie shook her head while wiping her face with her sleeve. "No. Not yet. We need to make the arrangements."

"Honey, are you sure?" said Jasmin. "That can certainly wait until tomorrow."

"No. I want...I *need* to get this over with. Please."

Jasmin glanced at Fionna before nodding. "Sure thing. Let's go over to Doc Smith's. He owns the local mortuary. I'll make sure we get a good deal on everything."

Torie sighed and allowed Fionna to help her to her feet, grateful for the comfort of the leather seats that cradled her once she was inside the car.

The trip to Elysian Fields, the funeral service owned by Doc Smith—who, as it turned out, was not a doctor of any kind, but simply kept the nickname he was given as a child because he was considered a know-it-all in class—was made in complete silence. Torie's face pressed against the window as she watched the world flash slowly by her.

"First, let me say that I am so sorry for your loss. I can't begin to imagine what you're feeling right now," said Doc Smith. He had cleared his other appointments for the afternoon so Torie and her friends had the funeral home to themselves. She wasn't exactly sure how to feel about that; granted, she had lost her mother, but everyone that came to a business like this had lost a loved one as well. Why should she take precedent over them? Still, selfish as it may have felt, she was grateful for the solitude inside the white Victorian that sat just off the main street of Singing Falls.

She nodded, swallowing hard and mumbled something about thanking the funeral director and all he was doing for her.

They settled into an office at the back of the home, a room with tasteful flower arrangements and a strategically placed box of Kleenex on a large desk that they gathered around.

After a minute of reflection, the funeral director leaned forward, his fingers interlocked on the desk as he addressed Torie.

"Have you thought about what kind of service your mother would want?"

Torie almost snorted. It hit her then that maybe she should have asked her mother what she wanted. She could still do that but decided against it. She shook her head instead, not trusting how her words might sound at that moment.

"Well, that's okay," he said, giving a quick look to Fionna and Jasmin. "Your mother was a special woman. I considered her a friend, and I grieve at her passing." He reached over and slid the box of tissues closer, sensing the conversation to come would be trying, to say the least.

"She would not want anything too grandiose," Torie said. "That wasn't who she was."

"No. It wasn't," Doc Smith echoed.

"Um, I also don't want her embalmed. I know she wouldn't have liked the thought of her body being pumped full of chemicals meant to preserve her."

The funeral director took out a pad and pen and began scratching out notes. "Of course. Whatever you think is best. That will mean a closed-casket celebration. You understand that, right?"

She nodded. It was weird that they considered this a celebration. What were they celebrating? The death of a loved one she would never have a chance to know; at least not in this lifetime. She knew that her friends would celebrate, but that was different. They knew her mother in this life, new her in a way that Torie did not. To them, she was a force of nature, her passing something to be remembered with reverence and awe.

But to Torie, she was just Mom.

"And what about her final resting vessel?" said Doc Smith. "Do you know what kind of casket you'd like for her final rest?"

What an odd way to put it, thought Torie. But she had to admit she had no idea. She had only been to one other funeral in her life; one of Ward's employees had been killed in a car accident on the expressway and she had attended the funeral with her then husband. That had brought out feelings of sorrow, but it was also something she had viewed from the outside; she had no idea what went in to creating the affair.

"Why don't you come with me?" Doc Smith said, extending a hand to Torie and leading her into a room with a multitude of caskets arranged along the walls. They were made of various materials; everything from solid, ornate wood all the way up to shiny titanium. Various interiors from velvet to shiny satin to tartan lined them, and the card placards placed before each told Torie the finished and interiors could be combined in any combination. Taken altogether, it was quite overwhelming.

"I don't mean to be crass," said Doc Smith, "but if there is a price point you are working within, I would be happy to steer you to where you might want to be."

Jasmin shot him a look and he averted his eyes, the slightest blush of crimson creeping into his cheeks.

"Well, to be honest," said Torie, "I hate to say it, but I'm...I mean, my cash reserves are not what they once were."

"Hush now," said Jasmin. "You don't worry about that." She

turned to the funeral director. "Money isn't a problem here. But Torie needs to find the one that is right for her mother. Don't look at the price tag."

Torie didn't say anything, just let her eyes feel their way around the space. She walked along, admiring the craft of the caskets and thinking how strange all of this was. That she was actually picking out something for the final resting place of someone she loved. In her time, she had furnished all their homes and had prided herself on her eye for picking the exact piece for each and every room.

But here, in this dimly lit room that tried unsuccessfully to be something other than what it was, she was at a loss.

Fionna took her hand. "It's okay. Take your time. You knew your mother; you know what she would like."

Did I? Torie thought. There was a time when she thought she knew her mother; but that was so long ago. That person was nothing like the woman she had just met only a couple of days prior.

She continued to walk around the space until her eyes lit on a casket that appeared to be made of a misty, blue metal, with polished steel rods and a silver insignia on the side. She walked slowly over to it and peered inside. There was a white satin interior with a small, matching pillow with just a bit of lace around the edges. As caskets go, it was quite beautiful and almost soothing in a strange way. She ran her hand along the polished surface, the metal cool and hard, almost like marble.

For some reason, she knew this was the one. It was perfect.

"This one," she said, turning to Doc Smith. "This is it."

"Excellent choice," he said, smiling softly.

"How much—" she started.

"Uh-uh," said Jasmin stepping up. "Don't ask that." She let her eyes play over the casket, nodding in approval. "It's perfect. Alva always did love this shade of blue."

"Well, if you're sure, then come have a seat; let's plan out the rest of the service. I have some paperwork for you to sign and we can be done with all of this."

For Torie, the rest of the ordeal was like walking through a dense fog; stumbling along, arms outstretched, afraid of bumping into something icky.

How many people were expected at the service? No idea.

Would she prefer a graveside ceremony, or would she like to reserve one of the beautiful halls in which to have the ceremony? No idea.

This brought her thoughts back around to open or closed casket. This was the one that gave her the most grief. That her mother was beloved she had no doubt. There was no trauma to the body, so that wasn't an issue with the viewing. No, it was just the thought of people, waiting in line to gawk at her mother.

No, not gawk; pay their respects.

She did not know these people in this tiny town that her mother had adopted. Or maybe that was the wrong way to think about it. They had adopted her. In many ways, as she was learning, they knew her mother on a much deeper level than Torie had ever imagined. Who was she to deny them final respects?

Fine. Open casket it would be. She would have to let the director know she changed her mind, as was her right.

Finally, after everything was decided, and the paperwork signed, she felt the tiniest bit of relief. Jasmin gave the director a card to charge everything to, and when Torie protested, she said she would hear none of that.

"Besides, it all comes from the same place," Jasmin had said.

"What? What do you mean?" Torie asked.

"Shh. There will be plenty of time for that later," Jasmin replied. "In the morning we will take you to the lawyer and get everything worked out."

Torie was confused, but before she could ask anything further, Doc Smith walked back in with a folder containing everything they had decided on. He handed it over to her with a heartfelt shake of her hand, and a slight smile that told her while it wasn't appropriate to give a full-blown smile in a time like this, it was enough to let her know that he was sorry for her loss. And even though she knew this was his business, she felt that he genuinely meant it.

As they left the funeral home and made their way to the car, Torie broke down one last time. Signing the paperwork to bury her mother meant it was final; it was real. Her mother was dead, and even though her ghost was still hanging out at her home, it was probably only a matter of time before that would be gone as well.

She was thankful for the handkerchief that Jasmin pulled out of the glove compartment and used it to dab at her eyes.

"I don't know how to thank you," Torie said, "and I don't know when or how, but I'm going to pay you back for this. With interest."

"Honey, you don't have to worry about that. Like I said, here in Singing Falls, we all drink from the same well."

"What does that even mean?" said Torie as she buckled her seatbelt.

"The finances. Here, as a member of our community, you don't have to worry about money. You're rich now."

Torie thought she must have misunderstood. Jasmin probably heard about her life before her husband came crashing down and ruined them, financially and personally.

"No, not anymore. I don't have access to that kind of money anymore."

"Not what you had in your old life," said Jasmin. "Here, you have inherited your family fortune. The income your mother was able to tap into...that every member of the community taps into. Being a member of a supernatural community that has existed for centuries has its perks. All our generational wealth is pooled into a single trust that funds the town and the people living here. You're set for life, Torie. And so is your son. Maybe, instead of waiting until tomorrow, we'll swing by the lawyer's office and get you set up now."

Torie was stunned, unsure how to react.

"Oh, but one thing," added Jasmin, "the lawyer is a vampire. And he has a thing for witches, so...watch your throat around him."

She threw her head back and roared in laughter as she peeled out of the parking lot.

# 14

The lawyer's office was yet another posh Victorian, this time right on Main Street. It was set back with a stone walkway that led to an impressive, forest-green double door. Once inside, the receptionist smiled politely and asked the women to have a seat while she walked into the back to let the firm's owner know there were visitors. Torie noticed a vase on the receptionist's desk that was filled with an array of what looked like dead sticks. Probably a vampire thing, and she was too emotionally worn out to inquire if she was right.

The fact that they were able to just walk right in impressed Torie. The lawyers she knew would never have allowed that; well, not unless you had them on a seven-figure retainer the way Ward once did.

The receptionist returned, her perma-smile fixed in place as she bade them to follow her into the back office. As soon as the door shut behind her, Jasmin placed both hands firmly on the desk of a short, lean man with round wire-rimmed glasses. She leaned in aggressively.

"What the hell, Arnold, we've just learned that vampires don't need an invite to enter someone's house? Is that true?"

His hesitation told them all the answer to that question.

"And who would have told you that?" Arnold said, his eyes wide behind the glasses. "Let me guess...you've been talking to those pesky dogs, haven't you?"

Jasmin rolled her eyes. "Not the point. The point is you were the one who told us vampires could only enter your home if you first invited them in."

"I might have overstated that," he said coyly, smiling at the witch. "But it was for your own peace of mind. I saw the way everyone in this town looked at me when I first arrived."

"Yeah, well, no more lies, okay? This town is built on trust."

Arnold nodded before slowly seeping his gaze over to Torie. "As you wish, Jasmin. Now, what can I do for you?"

"This is Alva's daughter, Torie," Jasmin said. "She needs to be set up."

At once, Arnold's demeanor changed. He stood, extending his hand to Torie in greeting. "I am so sorry to hear of your mother's passing. My thoughts are with you."

Was it still a 'passing' if the person was murdered? she wondered. She took his hand, noting it was both cold and hard; like a piece of steel that was covered in skin.

"Thank you," she said, instinctively raising a hand to her neck as she backed away.

Arnold smiled, his dark eyes wrinkling at the corners. "Let me guess, you were warned I have a predilection for witch's blood." He sighed, returning to his desk. "You make one confession during a game of truth or dare and look what happens..." He shot a glance at Jasmin. "And you, dear Fionna, you can come closer. I won't bite."

Torie noticed she was standing with her back pressed against the door, both arms clutching her purse in front of her. She narrowed her eyes and slowly walked over to stand next to Jasmin.

"So," said Arnold, "have a seat and let me pull up some information here."

Torie sat in the chair across from the large desk and watched as

Arnold's fingers danced across the keyboard of his laptop with blinding speed.

"So," he said finally, adjusting his glasses as he stared at the screen. He turned the laptop to face Torie. "As you can see, the house is yours; free and clear. All property taxes, and any monies needed for repairs will come out of the main fund of course. You also have been added to your mother's line of credit, and your name has been placed on her personal savings."

"Wait, what line of credit?" Torie asked. "I'm still a bit confused."

Arnold looked up at Jasmin.

"We told her the basics but figured it might be easier to see it for herself."

Arnold nodded. "Of course. For centuries, witches have been putting their money and assets into a central account. It started back during the great Salem witch trials where they never knew when they would need legal assistance to fend off the charges from the church; so they pooled their money, sharing it amongst themselves in the event one of them were charged with witchcraft.

"That continued from descendant to descendant. Until here we are today, with the initial account now valued at…well, it is considerable. So, over a century ago, this town was funded using that account. Everything a town typically relies on taxes to pay, are paid from this fund."

Torie's mind swam trying to imagine how such a thing was possible. She came from a wealthy background, but the amount of funding he was describing was beyond her ability to comprehend.

"On a personal note, your family, on your mother's side, has been passing down wealth for generations. They contribute to the greater fund, as all do, but they also have put aside money for all their descendant's to use. Everything in your mother's name now belongs to you."

He reached into his desk drawer and withdrew a silver key. Walking over to a large safe in the wall, he put the key into a lock, placed his thumb on the bio sensor, and turned the key. Reaching in, he withdrew a small box and walked back over to the desk.

Opening the box, he revealed a white credit card with no information printed on it. He then turned to a small table that sat against the back wall, where a three-dimensional printer sat. Keying in a command on his laptop, he opened a slot on the printer and dropped the card in. Instantly it was pulled into the printer, and two metallic rods appeared from the side, firing ruby-red lasers at the card. They whined and whirred, crisscrossing one another as they quickly engraved the card with a single, tiny barcode at the base. When finished, the card exited the printer through the same slit it had entered.

Arnold plucked the card and presented it to Torie.

"This now belongs to you. It is keyed to both your account and the town fund. It can only be used by you. The card will recognize your unique bio-rhythm and finger prints. I'll email you the link that will track any purchases and payments. Now, how else can I assist you?"

Torie was dumbfounded. "Well, what is the limit?"

"I don't know," said Arnold, puzzled. "No one has ever asked. I mean, the fund is well over nine figures and your personal share is... well, more than you could probably ever spend."

They sat there in silence while Torie got her bearings. "So, you're a real-life vampire, huh?"

Arnold nodded, not sure where she was going with that question. Torie looked at Jasmin who returned her stare blankly.

"If you're a vampire, why are you awake in the daylight?"

"Because I prefer to be awake during daytime hours with most everyone else. If you mean am I able to move about in sunlight; no. Direct sunlight will kill me."

"Oh," said Torie. She almost sounded dejected.

"It isn't him, Torie," said Jasmin. "I can promise you that."

Arnold looked at them, his brows furrowed.

Jasmin waved him off. "Forget it. I'll fill you in later."

"Well then," said Arnold, rising to escort them out of his office, "it has been a pleasure. I'm always at your service, ladies. Good day."

As soon as they were out of the building, Fionna gave a whole-bodied shudder, shaking her arms like a professional runner limbering up for a race.

"And what was wrong with you?" said Torie. "You barely spoke in there."

"Vampires give me the creeps," said Fionna. "It's hard to describe. As a squirrel shifter, I'm a prey animal. And vampires are apex predators; even higher up the food chain than wolves. Something about him triggers my flight or fight response; only with him it's more of a flight or stay in one spot and don't move response."

"And you," said Torie, turning to face Jasmin, "how do you know it's not him?"

"Because I know. He's been a part of this community for a very long time."

"How long?"

"Centuries. When he was human, he helped to hide accused witches during the Salem trials. He's been an ally from the beginning. So no, he has nothing to do with this."

"Maybe he can help us then?" Torie suggested.

Her friend shook her head. "No. Vampires don't get involved in our affairs. They stand above it. If he were to get involved, it would send a signal to his kind that we are accepting and welcoming to them. The last thing a town of witches and...prey shifters...need are more predators living among us. When he came out of the closet, so to speak, there was an uproar in this town. Many wanted him banished. It was your mother who called for cooler heads to prevail. And she was right. He's been a stand-up member of the community ever since."

Torie filed everything away in order to process it at a later date.

"Okay, c'mon. We need to hit the supermarket and the bakery. You'll be receiving visitors after the burial, so you need to stock up."

That was strange to Torie. The limited experience she had with funerals was that those who were not related to the deceased were the ones who brought by food. When she asked this, Fionna shook her head.

"No, that doesn't happen here. There are so many different types of supernaturals, someone will bring something to eat that will inevitably offend someone else. But if the person hosting the affair provides the food...well, no one is going to complain because they are there to provide support. But don't worry. You won't be doing it alone. We will all be there to help. As a matter of fact, you don't even have to do one single thing if you're not up for it."

Torie smiled and gave her friend a hug. Never in her four-plus decades on this earth had she known people like this.

No wonder her mother had been so drawn to this tiny town carved out in a huge mountain.

"Well, I do have a request," Torie said as they made their way to the car.

"Name it," said Jasmin.

"I think my mom would want me to have some of those elderberry pastries."

They laughed and climbed into the car, heading for the bakery.

THE SERVICE WAS EXACTLY what Torie's mother would have wanted. A small, intimate affair—if you could call a hundred-plus people intimate—without a lot of fanfare. Fionna had asked one of the wood nymphs to preside over the wake. Her words were lovely and made everyone at the ceremony smile as she recounted the many tales that involved Alva.

Hearing them, and the laughter they invoked, moved Torie to tears. Shawn had his arm around his mother and pulled close, fighting to hold back his own waterworks. They both wished they had spent more time with someone who had proved to be an amazing woman. Torie found herself hating her husband once again. It was his fault the rift between them had developed. It was his fault that Shawn had grown up not knowing his grandmother. She knew hatred would serve no purpose now, but for the moment, it warmed her in the early-morning, chilly mountain air.

As the coffin was lowered into the ground, the two of them stood graveside and tossed in two white roses that disappeared under two shovels of dirt, indicating the close of the graveside wake.

"Mom," said Shawn, "can I ask you something?"

"Of course, baby. What is it?"

The young man standing next to her swallowed hard. "If Gram was so happy here, and so beloved by all these people; why would she kill herself?"

Torie turned to look up into the sad face of her son.

"Your grandmother did not kill herself. I...I don't know what happened, but I know she didn't do that. I won't have you believing that."

"I didn't think that was what happened. Is that what you're doing with Fionna and the others? Trying to figure out what happened?"

Torie knew she had to be careful here. As much as she wanted her son close, she also wanted him on a plane back to Austin as soon as possible. She had already made arrangements to meet with Arnold the vampire again; to set up an ironclad will to make sure Shawn was taken care of in the event something happened to her.

"I need to find the truth here, Shawn. And who knows? Maybe I'll stick around for a while."

Shawn looked at his mother and smiled. "I think that's a good idea, Mom. You know, if you want, I'll stay and help. Looks like Gram had a lot of stuff in that house to go through."

Torie reached up and brushed a strand of hair away from her child's face. *Kids these days and their shaggy hair.*

"No. You go back to school. I need to do this. It will be good for me to spend some time with my memories."

"Okay. If you're sure, I'll head back tomorrow."

She took his hand and patted it. "I'm absolutely sure. You'll just be gone for a few more weeks and then you can come back for break. How's that?" Plus, if she was lucky, that would give her time to solve a murder. Shawn smiled and walked away, heading for her car, keys in hand.

Jasmin, Fionna and Taylor fell into step with Torie as she walked along.

"So," said Jasmin, "did you get what we needed?"

"I sure did," Taylor replied with a bright smile, holding up her digital camera. She had asked to photograph the burial for the local paper, and everyone had thought that was a marvelous idea.

"Investigation one-oh-one," said Jasmin. "The killer usually can't resist being close to their victims one last time. They always show up at the funeral...and now, we have pics of everyone here. Time to unmask a monster."

## 15

Torie had never been so thankful for a large kitchen island in her life. It was covered in dishes and platters; cheeses, grapes, shrimp, casseroles, breads of all kinds, turkeys, hams, and more cakes and pies than she had ever seen outside of a bakery.

True to their word, Fionna, Taylor, Glen and Jasmin had done the majority of the work. Many of the shops had donated food, refusing to take money for the celebration that marked the passing of a beloved community member. Torie walked among strangers, shaking hands and receiving condolences, while wondering if she had just shaken the hand of the person who had killed her mother.

She was also afraid that her mother would make an appearance. But that didn't happen. She only seemed to be present when Torie called for her. Part of her had wanted her mother to see the turnout; to know what she meant to so many. Fionna and Jasmin had advised against that.

The dead still had feelings, they said, and this might be enough to send her mother's spirit into a depression.

It was an exhausting afternoon, with many people recounting their favorite encounters with Alva, and asking Torie to do the same. Every time that came up, her eyes would brim with tears and the person asking would just give her a hug, tell her it was okay, and thankfully move on.

After meeting each person, Jasmin would sidle up to her and whisper in her ear what supernatural camp the person was from. There were myriad wood elves, nymphs, fairy folk, and shifters of all kinds.

"What about witches?" Torie asked. "Are there more of them around?"

"Correction," said Jasmin with a smile, "you mean more of us. Not many. There are still a few in the area, but they will be holding their own vigil for Alva. Witches are very private. You'll meet them as time goes by. But the death of one of our kind is a very traumatic thing."

Torie understood all of this only too well.

"So have you picked up on anything?" Fionna asked, appearing at their side. Taylor was with her and they both leaned in, eager for any updates.

"Well, maybe if you had let me do what I needed to," said Jasmin, "we would know something by now."

"What does that mean?" asked Torie.

"She wanted to poison the food," said Taylor.

"Not poison," Jasmin quickly amended, "just lace some of it with a potion that would have acted like a truth serum. Add to it some powder that would have loosened lips and I'm betting the killer would have revealed themselves by now."

Fionna tsked, her face a mask of disapproval. "You have no idea how that would have affected so many of the supernaturals here. Can you imagine the secrets some of them might be keeping? You would have forced all of that into the open."

Jasmin grumbled but didn't reply.

"Imagine if you were pressed to suddenly unload some of the secrets you carry around," said Fionna, fixing her gaze on her friend.

"Whatever. It was just an idea."

Before anyone could say anything, Torie felt a tap on her shoulder and turned to see the young receptionist from Arnold's law firm standing behind her. She was holding a large bouquet of flowers and offered them to Torie.

"Arnold sends his condolences," she said. "He said to let you know that he is very sorry he can't be here in person for you."

"Thank you," said Torie, taking the flowers. "They are beautiful." And they really were; an assortment of calla lilies and baby's breath. "I'll find some water for them."

"Got it," said Taylor, taking the flowers from her and heading off towards the back of the room.

"Oh…thank you," Torie called after the young shifter before turning back to Arnold's receptionist. "So…I'm sorry I didn't get your name."

"Breonna. And if there is anything I can do for you, please don't hesitate to let me know."

"Of course, Breonna. What a beautiful name. Give Arnold my thanks, will you?"

Breonna stood there, not moving. "First time at a funeral?" Torie asked.

Breonna nodded, looking around. "It isn't as solemn and sad as I expected."

"That's because we are remembering a person's life," said Jasmin, "not mourning their death."

Breonna seemed to think about this for a moment before nodding and offering an awkward smile.

"Here, let me take that coat," said Jasmin, "you must be melting in it. Stay and have some refreshments."

The girl jumped, clutching her shearling jacket closer around her, clasping the collar tight around her neck. "No, it's okay. I have been fighting off a cold and…well, I need to get back to the office. But I'll give your regards to Arnold." She nodded again, almost a bow, and headed back through the room of guests towards the front door.

"What an odd little girl," said Tori.

Jasmin shrugged. "She's a child. They're all odd at that age."

Torie elbowed her in jest. "Hey, we were that age once."

"Ugh. Don't remind me. Reminds me of a saying: 'Youth is wasted on the young.' Or something like that."

They both laughed and headed back into the kitchen.

"So," said Torie, "how long will this last? Not that I mind of course…"

Jasmin held up a hand to silence her. "Don't say another word. It's time to clear everyone out. Leave that to us."

She called to Taylor and Fionna and said something to them that Torie couldn't quite make out. They each spread out and started speaking with the guests. Slowly, the crowd thinned, and the clamor of voices receded, dying down from a din to a whisper, and finally to silence as the last of the visitors took their leave.

Freya was the last to come up to Torie, her sad smile filled with concern for her friend. She threw her arms around her and gripped her close.

"Are you sure you don't want to come back to the city with me? I feel strange leaving you here all alone. Especially now that I know Shawn will be leaving as well."

"Thank you, my friend," said Torie, "but I am just fine. And I'm not alone. Plus, I promise that if it gets to be too hard on me here, you'll be the first to know. Cos I'll be knocking on your door."

"Anytime," Freya said. "The door is always open for you." She turned to Torie's new friends and smiled. "Take care of her. She's one of a kind."

"Oh, trust me, we know," said Fionna, returning the smile.

She walked her old friend to the door and hugged her one last time, waving as she climbed into her car and eased out of the drive.

"Whew," she said, turning to the few people that remained. "I can't thank you enough for that. There is no way I could have done that without you."

Glen had taken it upon herself to usher the last of the guests out and was directing the mass of cars out of the driveway and onto the road. Fionna, Jasmin and Taylor were already in the kitchen tidying up. In the large island cabinetry, there were two entire drawers dedicated to Tupperware. Torie laughed as Jasmin struggled to find tops that matched the bottoms. Witch or mortal, it seemed neither could escape the mystery of the vanishing Tupperware lids. Eventually, the granite top of the island came into view as food was cleared away.

The stainless-steel dishwasher was whirring along quietly, and the last of the desserts had been covered with foil. That was when they all sat down at the island, glad to be off their feet.

Jasmin began to remove one of her shoes but then looked at Torie for approval before proceeding. Torie laughed and nodded, reaching to remove hers as well.

"Thank God," she said, "my feet are killing me. They are going to be the size of watermelons tomorrow."

"Coconut oil," said Taylor.

"What?" asked Torie.

"Coconut oil. It cures everything from aches and pains to burns. Oh, and it's the best lube around if you ever need—"

"Girl, please," said Jasmin, cutting her off. "We get the picture."

"I'm just saying," said Taylor. "And knowing your mother, I'm sure there is some around here."

That brought a laugh from all of them.

Glen walked into the kitchen and smiled at the ladies. "Well, that's the last of them. Unless you need me to stay, I have a shift I picked up tonight. You okay if I leave?"

She said it to them all, but Torie answered.

"Thank you for everything Glen. I mean that. But I think we are all good."

Glen nodded and walked over to Fionna and gave her a kiss.

"See you later," Fionna called after her.

"Would you ladies like a drink?" asked Torie. "Whiskey, beer or wine? Sorry, if you want to mix up a Cosmo or something that is on you."

"Whew, no," said Jasmin, "you know we can't be drinking all that sugar. I'll take a whiskey."

"Wine for me," said Fionna.

"Same here," said Taylor.

Jasmin took out the glasses and set them in front of her friends before going to the liquor cabinet and removing a bottle of Rye and a Cabernet. They sat there in silence, enjoying the warmth that came from friendship and spirits.

"So, what do you think?" said Fionna to no one in particular.

"I think that whoever killed Alva was probably here in this room," said Jasmin. "We have a record of everyone now, so we start going through them, one by one. Eliminate as we go until we find the bastard who did this."

"What are you suggesting we do?" asked Taylor. "Interview each and every person?"

"If need be, yes," said Jasmin. "It will be tedious, but I know a spell of revelation that will help to identify lies. And don't worry, it doesn't involve drugging anyone."

"Can you teach it to me?" asked Torie.

Everyone stared at her in silence. Slowly, Jasmin nodded.

"Good. I want to learn everything I can about being a witch. Including how to use my powers. My mother said I would find a teacher. Is that you?"

Jasmin looked around. "Well, I don't see any other witches here, so I guess that answers your question." She turned her gaze to Fionna and Taylor. "And I'll need your help to teach her."

"Us?" said Taylor. "What can we do to help? We don't know the first thing about magic."

"That's true, but you can do something I can't; shift. And Alva said whatever Torie's innate magical skill is, it centers around her ability to talk to shifters in their animal form. That's something I will be on the outside of."

"Oh, I get it," said Fionna. "Whatever kind of witch she is, it centers around shifters."

"Exactly, and that skill will come in very handy for someone tracking a shifter killer. The sooner we can unlock it, the better. Also, the sooner we can start teaching you some magic, the safer you'll feel. Or at least the safer I'll feel about you."

"Sounds like a plan," said Torie. "When do we start?"

"When does Shawn leave?" Jasmin questioned.

Torie checked her watch. "He's on the last flight out tonight. So, we'll need to get him to the airport in a couple of hours."

"Then that's when we start; as soon as you get back. One thing; when you hear the voice of a shifter, does it sound like their regular voice, and do you actually hear it with your ears or is it in your mind?"

Torie thought for a second. "I'm not sure. I've never heard Eddie's human voice, so I don't know what he sounds like. And, honestly, I guess I didn't pay attention to where the sound came from."

"Interesting," came a deep, guttural voice from the workroom. They heard footsteps coming through the patio doors and turned just as Max stepped into the kitchen. Standing next to him was Elric, in wolf form. He was large, but lean, his back coming up to Max's waist. Max reached down and ruffled his fur.

"Drop it," growled Max.

Elric obeyed and leaned forward to gingerly let something fall from his mouth into a dark heap on the floor.

As one, the women gasped. It was Eddie. And he wasn't moving.

## 16

Before any of them could react, Taylor shifted into her fox form and placed herself between the women and the wolves. Her thick hair stood on edge, her tail bristled as she growled in warning.

"Havath un-to," shouted Jasmin, holding one hand out to her side. Instantly, a large butcher knife freed itself from the block in which it was stored and flew to her grasp. She held the blade before her. "Get the hell away from him!" she waved the knife menacingly at the two of them. "Or I swear, blood be damned, I will cut you deep!"

Torie looked at her appreciatively. "You have got to teach me that one."

Max raised both hands and stepped slowly back. He looked down at Elric and gave him an almost imperceptible nod. In the blink of an eye, the wolf was gone and the man appeared, standing next to his alpha.

"Easy, Jasmin," he said, "we aren't here to cause trouble."

Fionna and Jasmin gasped, and it was only then that he remembered he was naked. His hands dropped in front of him, shielding himself from their view. Torie rushed into the living room, snatched a throw from the back of the love seat and brought it to him. He sheepishly wrapped it around his waist, avoiding her eyes as he did. Max gave his subordinate a look that, to Torie's eye, seemed borderline disapproving.

"Why are you naked?" queried Jasmin in dismay.

"Um, I left my clothes back in the woods. When we shift, they get all messed up..." Elric said sheepishly.

"Taylor?" said Jasmin.

In response, the fox shifted back to human form, fully clothed.

"Hey, how do you—" Elric started before Max elbowed him in the ribs.

"Forget that," said Fionna, "what have you done to Eddie?" Despite her innate fear of the wolves, she ran to the black cat's side and carefully picked him up. He was breathing, but just barely.

"We didn't do anything to him," said Max. "We found him on a ridge a couple of miles from here. He was exactly as you see him now. I swear."

They hurried to the workroom and laid him on the table. He seemed frail, and thinner than he had looked the last time Torie had seen him, but other than that, he just seemed to be in a deep sleep.

"So what?" said Jasmin, still brandishing the knife. "We're just supposed to believe you found him and carried him back here?" She placed one hand gently on his side and ran it along his fur.

"What are you looking for?" asked Max. His tone told them he already knew what she was going to say.

"Bite marks," Jasmin replied, her gaze locked on Max's.

"Told you," said Max, looking over at Elric.

"Jasmin, he's telling the truth. We didn't hurt him. He was like that when we found him."

"Why would he be up in the ridges?" asked Fionna. "All shifters know to stay in town while this psychopath is still free."

"No idea," said Max. "But after leaving here, I found a scent out back. Near where the vet was killed. And layered in with that scent, was a cat shifter. So I reached out to El here and we followed it. Tracked it up to the ridges and sure enough, found him there. Just lying out on the rocks like he was sunbathing or something."

"All we could think to do was bring him back here; see if maybe you could help him."

"Without Ellie, there isn't much we can do," said Taylor. "There's another vet in Trinity, but...you know what she is like."

"Yeah. If you're bringing that one up, we're outta here," said Max. "Bad blood with the Trinity bunch."

"Wait," said Fionna, as she dug into her pockets, taking out her phone. Her fingers played across it as she sent a text. "Glen might be able to help. Granted, this isn't a human, but still, she's a nurse. Maybe she can do something. I told her to grab her emergency kit and get back over here ASAP."

"In the meantime," said Max, "you wanna put that knife away?"

Jasmin narrowed her gaze at him before glancing over at Torie, who just nodded in agreement.

"Fine," she said, sending the knife flying back to its place, nestled in with the rest of the set. "And just so you know, even without the knife...you try anything, I still got something for your ass." She snapped her fingers and sparks flew from the tips.

"So I see," said Max, appreciatively.

Torie moved into the kitchen, getting out some clean towels and filling a pot with water.

"What are you doing?" asked Fionna.

"I don't know," she replied, "but every medical drama I've seen they always need clean linen and boiled water. Figured I might as well have it ready."

"Um, yeah, if he were about to give birth," mumbled Jasmin.

A short time later the door sprang open and Glen rushed in, wearing her blue hospital scrubs and carrying a black and red backpack slung over one shoulder.

"What is it? What happened?" she asked, looking around desperately for Fionna.

"It's okay, babe," Fionna said. "We're all fine. I'm sorry about your shift. But we need you in here." She led her to the workroom and showed her Eddie.

Glen looked at him and then back at Fionna.

"Is that...Eddie?"

"Yes," said Torie. "He was found like this. Can you help him?"

"I...I don't know what I can do," Glen said, moving to stand next to the cat. "I mean, I'm not a veterinarian. I don't know anything about animal anatomy."

She took a stethoscope from her bag, placed the ends in her ears and then eased the receptive end onto Eddie's chest.

"I mean, his heart rate seems strong; slow, but steady. There's nothing in his chest that I can hear, but...I don't really know what I'm listening for. Do you have any clean towels?"

"Ah ha," said Torie, running back into the kitchen. "I knew you'd need these. I also have some hot water on if you need that."

Glen smiled. "Thank you. But this will do for now." She took one of the towels and laid it under Eddie's head and then used the corner of the other to open one of his eyes. She peered closely and repeated the act with the other eye.

"His pupils look like a cat's...but I just don't know."

"Well, there has to be something you can do," said Fionna.

"This would be a lot easier if he were human. At least then I'd know what to look out for."

Jasmin snapped her finger, which caused both Max and Elric to jump.

"Maybe that could be arranged."

"What do you mean?" asked Fionna. "Can you turn him human?"

"To my knowledge it hasn't been done before," said Jasmin. "There is no spell I know that can make a shifter turn. But..." she looked at Torie and smiled. "Maybe between us, we can get him to do it."

"What do you mean? What can I do? Maybe I should call on Mom?" Torie asked.

Jasmin shook her head. "The old Alva...yes. But this after-life version is not the witch she once was. You said that Eddie spoke to you, that you can hear his voice. Well, what if part of your magic is some form of telepathy? Maybe that's what allows you to communicate with them in animal form. If that's true, then maybe that connection works both ways. Maybe I can send your thoughts into his mind. What if Eddie is in there, but just unconscious…or stuck."

"You said the longer a shifter stays in animal form, the more like that animal they become," Torie said, turning to Fionna.

Fionna's eyes lit up. "Yes! That's right. What if he just doesn't remember how to become human again?"

"You, wolves," said Jasmin, turning to Max and Elric, "what is the longest you've been in wolf form?"

Elric started to speak but a look from Max cut him off.

"I'm not sure that is true," said Max. "In our case, we are born in our wolf form, and then, as we age, we turn human. From what I have heard, that is not the case with all other shifters." He eyed Taylor, giving the fox a smile.

"Werewolves are different," said Taylor, "that is true. But for the rest of us, we are born in human form. Then our parents teach us how to shift at an early age. But they do warn us about the dangers of staying in animal form."

"So what do we do?" said Torie. She was anxious to help, tired of being on the sidelines watching the game from afar.

"I'm going to perform a spell that will place your mind inside Eddie's. Once the connection is made, you have to speak to him, remind him that he can become human again…that he needs to be human."

"Okay. What do you need me to do in order to make this work?"

"Just open your mind to me and to Eddie. Remember, once I cast your consciousness into his, you will experience his reality as yours. Don't get lost. Also, your innate magical gifts may start to kick in and try to fight back. Resist that urge; you need to go with the flow." She turned to face Glen. "When this happens…*if* it happens, and he shifts, you'll have to move fast. Do whatever you need to in order to keep him human."

Glen nodded and began to root through her backpack, taking out a small bottle and a hypodermic syringe.

"Torie, are you sure you're willing to do this?" asked Fionna. "Jasmin, is there any possibility Torie could be hurt during this?"

"I have no idea," replied the witch. "Never done anything close to this before. For all we know, nothing will happen."

"Look, I want to do this," said Torie. "I trust all of you; and I want to help. Whatever it takes."

"Okay, can you...is there enough room on the table for you to lie next to Eddie?"

Taylor and Fionna carefully moved Eddie closer to the edge of the table, clearing as much room next to him as possible. Torie grunted as she heaved herself onto the table, lying on her back next to the cat.

"Okay," said Jasmin, "try to relax and let your mind go as blank as possible. Don't focus on anything other than the sound of my voice."

Torie nodded and closed her eyes. She wasn't sure how she was supposed to think of nothing, but she imagined herself as a small rock; something that was untouched by everything around her. Feelings, emotions, thoughts...all of it rolled off her smooth surface. She tried to imagine how she felt in the last five minutes of her yoga classes when the instructor told them all to find peace and serenity.

*Namaste*, she thought, *make my mind a rock.*

Somewhere, Jasmin began to chant, and her voice seemed to come from above Torie and all around her at the same time.

> *"Spirits of my ancestors, guide my heart*
> *as I peel back the layers of cloud and dark.*
> *Daughter of the moon, and sister of the sun,*
> *I implore you now, make these two minds one!"*

*What kind of Endora, backwoods Bewitched spell is that?* thought Torie, but then, before she could question it, she felt like someone had just fired her out of a giant slingshot.

Once, she had accompanied Ward to the Sears Tower and made the mistake of looking down from the observation deck. The sense of vertigo she experienced then was nothing to the complete loss of orientation she now felt. Even though she knew she was lying on her back, she felt everything around her spin to the point that she had no idea what was up and what was down.

She wanted to vomit, but then she felt the cooling touch of hands on her legs and shoulders. Her friends were her anchor and it served not only to reassure her they were there for her, but it also reminded her of her purpose. She forced herself to take deep breaths and concentrate on projecting a single name in her mind: Eddie.

She had no idea what she was doing but figured the feeling she was experiencing was her slipping into his mind. Maybe he would be able to hear her. She called again and again, until she heard a single sound, a meow, in response.

*There you are*, she thought, angling her mind in the direction the sound came from. In her mind's eye, she saw him; a small, frightened kitten, cowering in place. He was so tiny, and she could feel the fear radiating off him.

"It's okay," she whispered. "Here, let me help you. Just like before."

She bent over and scooped up the kitten, stroking it reassuringly.

"Aren't you just the most precious thing? But you know that you can't stay like this, don't you?"

She heard another meow in response, but this time, the squeak sounded more like the cry of a baby than that of a cat.

"That's right, Eddie," she said. "You're hurting and you're scared. But there are a lot of people here that want to protect and help you. But we can't do that with you in the shape you're in. I need you to do something for me...okay?"

The kitten in her mind nodded slowly, looking up at her with bright eyes.

"I...I can try," came a small voice from inside the cat.

"Good. Now that we've made contact, I don't know what I'm supposed to do next, other than to tell you that you need to shift back to human form."

The kitten looked confused for a moment.

"Eddie," she said, this time her voice was sterner. It was the voice she had used on Shawn over the years to make him clean up his Legos and eat anything green on his plate. "Eddie, turn back into a human. Now!"

Then, as quickly as she had been sucked into his mind, she was expelled. She imagined it was what it felt like to be shot out of a torpedo tube. One minute she was mentally admonishing a tiny feline, and the next she was opening her eyes, the ceiling of her mother's workroom coming into focus.

She moaned and turned her head to one side. To her shock, she was no longer lying next to a cat, but rather was now face to face with a very handsome man whose eyes blinked slowly, taking her in.

## 17

"Mom, what's going on?"

Torie froze, her eyes growing wide as she looked around to see Shawn standing in the doorway to the workspace, his face a mask of questions.

"Oh, hi, baby...I thought you were upstairs packing," Torie said, trying to sound nonchalant.

"Well, I was. I'm all set, and just came down for a snack and to see what time you wanted to leave." He walked slowly into the room, glancing at the man on the table his mother had been lying next to. "Who's that?"

"Oh, that's Eddie. He's um...my friend."

Shawn looked from Eddie to the women around him, and finally settled on the two wolves, his eyebrows shooting up as he took in Elric's form; naked except for the blanket wrapped around his waist.

"And...who are they?" he added. "Mom, what's going on?"

"We were...um, we were..." she began.

"We were rehearsing," said Jasmin quickly. "For a little improv play we are going to put on at the community theater next week."

"Yes," said Torie, thinking quickly, "and we're going to film it and put it on Facebook. It's a play about women over forty reclaiming their sexuality. Oh...hey, we need someone to work the iPhone when we go to shoot the final cut. Maybe you could—"

Shawn held up a hand in front of his horrified face. "I'm out. Nope, I don't even want to hear anymore." He placed two fingers in his ears and quickly ran out of the room. Once the fear and rush of adrenaline left her, Torie began to laugh hysterically.

Fionna laughed with her. "Oh my Goddess, did you see the look on his face?"

"That was fast thinking, Jasmin, thank you," said Torie.

"Not as fast as yours," she replied. "You added the icing to that cake."

This made them laugh even harder. Only the wolves weren't laughing.

"What's so funny?" asked Elric. "I don't get it." To which another round of laughter erupted, causing the two wolves to look questioningly at one another.

"Okay, enough of that," said Jasmin, wiping at her eyes. She walked over to Eddie and placed a hand on his forehead. "Eddie, are you okay? How are you feeling?"

"I feel like I've run a marathon and I have the mother of all headaches." His voice was raspy and weak. He tried to sit up but a rush of dizziness made him instantly regret trying. He plopped back on the table with a thud.

"Don't try to move just yet," said Glen, rushing over to his side. She placed two fingers on his wrist and looked at her watch while she counted his heartbeat. "Low, and a little thready." Taking out a pen, she aimed it at his eyes, clicking on a light that she waved in and out of his field of vision. "You could have a slight concussion, and you're definitely dehydrated. You need water."

Taylor immediately ran back into the kitchen and filled a cup before bringing it back to her friend.

"Not too much at once," said Glen, taking it from his hands before he could down the entire thing. Again she rummaged through her bag, retrieving the needle she had hidden in there when Shawn showed up unexpectedly.

"This is a mild sedative. It's going to help you get some healthy sleep, so you can keep healing."

"Wait," said Jasmin, stopping her from driving the syringe into his arm, "we need to ask him about what happened."

"Ask whatever you want," said Glen, "but I'm administering this sedative before he gets worse. It's either that or you let me take him to the hospital."

Jasmin looked at her and then stepped back as she gave him a quick jab with the needle.

"Eddie," said Jasmin after Glen had moved from his side, "can you tell us what happened to you the night you were attacked?"

His eyes grew glassy as he regarded her. He smiled, feeling the effects of the drugs.

"I wish I could. I...don't remember."

"What do you mean you don't remember?" Fionna asked as she moved in closer. "You were attacked, but you survived."

"I wish I could. I feel like...there is something there, but I can't quite grasp it. Whoa...how did you do that, Fionna? How did you make two of you?"

And then, with that last slur of words, he passed into unconsciousness, his head lolling to one side.

"I'll get a pillow for him," offered Taylor, heading off to the living room.

"I thought it wasn't good for people with a concussion to sleep," said Torie.

"Normally it isn't," replied Glen. "But in the case of a shifter, they heal differently, and faster, than humans. Sleeping will let his body recover and his innate abilities as a shifter to heal his wounds quicker; even in human form."

Torie took a deep breath and turned to face the wolves.

"Okay, talk," she said, steeling her voice and narrowing her eyes. "You know something, don't you?"

"What are you talking about?" asked Jasmin.

"When I was inside Eddie's mind, I sensed something. Something that had traumatized him. He was running from something, something that hunted him. He was in mortal fear for his life." She turned and faced Fionna. "The kind of fear someone would have if they thought they were about to be eaten."

Fionna hissed, stepping away from the wolves.

"Fionna, I told you, we had nothing to do with this," said Elric.

"So you keep saying," said Torie. "But that doesn't mean you—or rather *he*—doesn't know something." She turned her gaze to Max, pinning him in place.

Jasmin turned on the wolf. She whispered an incantation that Torie couldn't make out and her hand became engulfed in blue flames.

"If you are hiding something from us, wolf, I suggest you spill it now...before I have to make you talk."

Max growled as the woman approached. His mouth filled with razor sharp teeth and his face changed slightly to more wolfen features as he retreated from the magic.

"I told you, witch, we didn't do it. Yes, maybe there was another scent we picked up along with your cat friend's here, but I swear I don't know what it was. It was a creature we are not familiar with."

"Keep going," said Jasmin, slowly dousing the brightness of her magical flame.

"It was the scent of a predator," said Max. "That was why we followed it. To see what had invaded this town...what was hunting your shifters. But there was a problem with the scent that confused us."

"A problem? What was it?" questioned Torie.

Max didn't say anything, his nose, now elongated and more canine-like, quivered as he took in the scents around him.

"It was shielded by magic," said Elric, breaking the silence.

The women stared at him, unsure of what to say.

"That's a lie," spat Jasmin. Her anger made her voice quiver as she advanced on the beta wolf.

"No, it isn't," said Max. He struggled to regain control of himself, pushing the wolf away and presenting only his human face. "It's true. We could not discern the scent of the creature that was committing the crime because it was cloaked in magic. Trust me, it's a smell we have become very acquainted with."

"Why can't he be telling the truth?" said Torie. She was looking at Elric, and something instinctual told her he was not lying.

"Because what they are saying is that a witch is behind these killings," said Fionna quietly.

"And that isn't possible," echoed Jasmin, her voice cold as steel.

"Why not?" said Max. "You were quick to believe that we were the culprits. Why couldn't it be one of your cauldron-stirring brethren?"

He raised his arms in protection as Jasmin advanced on him, death in her eyes.

"Stop it," said Torie, stepping between them. "There will be no fighting in this house."

Jasmin stopped out of respect for her friend. Then she turned to Torie.

"They are trying to get us to turn on one another. They want us to fight amongst ourselves so we can't see the real culprit."

"And what good would that do us?" asked Max. "We want whoever is doing this to be captured just as much as you do."

"Oh yeah," said Jasmin, "why would that be? Give me one plausible reason."

"Because we are tired of running and we have no place else to go," blurted Elric. "We just...want to belong."

Max growled at his subordinate, baring his human teeth in the process. "Be quiet, beta."

"No," said Torie, stepping forward. "He has every right to speak up, just as you do." She wasn't sure where her bravado came from, but in her gut she felt that it was the right thing to say.

No one spoke as Elric reluctantly continued. "You know that we are new here in town. From day one we heard the rumors that there was a serial killer stalking this town, and we knew the dangers of being the new guys. But we came up from Trinity, and if you knew what we had been through there...well, let's just say that the chance to start over in a place that values everyone equally... called to us."

His eyes were focused on the floor as he spoke, and Torie had the feeling that he was speaking only the truth.

*"We have done bad things, in defense of ourselves, but we have never hurt an innocent."*

This last statement she heard in her head. It was Elric's voice, but he had definitely not spoken it aloud. She looked at him, and he was staring hard at her; his gray eyes pleading with her. She looked at the women around her, just to be certain that no one else had heard.

"Is it really out of the realm of possibility?" Torie said. "I mean, shouldn't we consider that anyone could be a suspect?"

"You have yet to come into your power," said Jasmin. "Because if you had, you would know that all Hexes are defenders of life; we protect and serve. That's all."

"Not all of you," said Max, softly. "I've seen first-hand what some of you are capable of." He lifted his shirt, showing long, raised burn marks that scarred his torso. "This is from a witch who channeled hellfire through her whip." He then bent over and pulled up a pant leg to show a deformed calf muscle that looked like it had been torn away then half glued back on again. "And this is from a witch who kept me in enchanted silver chains...just to see how long it might take me to gnaw off my own leg to get free."

No one spoke, and Torie had to fight back the threat of tears.

"Well," said Jasmin quietly, "I don't know what kind of witches you've encountered but I guarantee that no one here in Singing Falls would ever do something like that."

"But that's just it," said Max, "you don't know what kinds of witches are out there. Yeah, sure, here in this town everyone is all kumbaya and pixie dust...but you drive down to Trinity and see what your sisters have been up to down there." He turned away, his face red with a combination of embarrassment and anger. "I'm just saying. Not everyone welcomes supernaturals with open arms and a plate full of elderberry muffins."

"Fair enough," said Jasmin. Then she swallowed hard. "For what it's worth, I'm sorry. You should never have to experience what you've been through; and anyone who would do this to you...I refuse to call them a sister."

Max didn't respond, but Torie could tell from the way his shoulders relaxed that he felt better and accepted Jasmin's apology.

"We just want to help you catch this person," said Elric. "We like it here."

"Okay, so now we are opening up the search to witches as well," said Taylor.

"Well, the good thing about that is, there are only a few here in town," added Fionna. "Present company excluded, we should be able to pay them a visit within a day and see what we can find out."

"Does anyone else find it suspicious that Eddie doesn't remember what happened to him?" Torie asked. When no one answered, she rolled her eyes. "That is the same thing my mother said; she couldn't remember what had happened to her. From what I can tell, she isn't senile...or rather, wasn't. She said there was a hole in her memories... and that is kind of what Eddie hinted at."

Jasmin nodded, deep in thought. "Maybe there is something there. Add that fact to what the wol...er...Max and Elric told us, maybe this is magical in nature."

"You mean a spell that creates amnesia?" said Taylor.

"Not a spell," said Jasmin. "If that were the case, I would be able to sniff that out. But there are more mundane ways to create the same affect."

"Medication," said Glen. "You think that someone gave them something?"

"That would open the door to a lot of other professionals then," noted Torie.

"Maybe not," replied Glen. "The hospital is really the only place that would carry the kind of drugs that can do that. There is a master database that shows all medication inventory, who checked it out, and they cross reference to the patient it was used on. I can check that and see if any of it is unaccounted for."

Fionna frowned. "I don't know. Whoever is doing this has no

problem murdering shifters. I don't want you in their cross-hairs in any way."

"And I appreciate that," said Glen, "but you are out here risking your life for people in your community. Well, you're my people, and I am not sitting on the sidelines just because I'm human. I love you, and if there is something I can do to help, you damn well better know I'm going to do it."

Something she said struck a nerve with Torie. "I want in as well. I'm the newbie in town, but I want to do my part."

"Very well," said Jasmin. "If you're okay with calling a share ride for your son, there is something we need to do."

Torie didn't like the idea of not driving her son to the airport, but she knew there was a greater good to be performed.

"Of course," she said. "What are we doing?"

"We are going to follow another lead. Down in Trinity."

Everyone except Torie began to voice their concern. Torie raised her hand to silence the group and looked at Jasmin with narrowed eyes. "Okay, maybe it's time you told me just what it is about Trinity that has everyone so freaked out. And what exactly is it we are going to do there?"

Jasmin grinned. "Ellie's body was taken there for autopsy, just as your mother's was. Her wounds would have been harder to classify; they wouldn't be able to just brush it off like they did your mother's. We are going there to find her body and her clothes and see if we can find out what she might have known that got her killed alongside your mother."

Max stepped up at the mention of Trinity.

"If you're going to that hell pit, you're not going alone. Take Elric with you. I'll go with the woman to the hospital to snoop around for drugs."

"Medication," corrected Glen.

"Yes. Medication," Max continued. "The squirrel shifter is right; you start poking around in a killer's business, you might show up on their hit list. I'll keep her safe, I promise."

"Okay," said Torie. "Sounds like we have a plan. Do we head out now, while it's still daylight? Or do we wait for nightfall?"

Jasmin laughed. "You really don't know about Trinity Cove, do you? There is no daylight there…it's a town that has been taken over by a supernatural darkness. Imagine Alaska during their winter when the sun doesn't come up…if Alaska were run by werewolves, demons and vampires."

## 18

Torie decided if they were venturing into a real-life hellmouth, they weren't doing it on an empty stomach. She whipped up a lunch using whatever she could find in the refrigerator. It turned out to be a surprisingly good pasta salad with fresh tomato bruschetta.

"So, when did a rich girl like you ever learn to cook like this?" Jasmin quizzed.

"Ha. Well, I may have indulged in a cleaning crew from time to time, but I never allowed us to have a cook. Dinner was special to me; the one time of the day that all of us sat down together. I made it a point to always prepare everything from scratch. Ward used to chide me for it, but Shawn loves my cooking." She reached over and ruffled his hair.

"Ward sounds like an ass," said Elric between bites.

Shawn stopped mid-chew, looking up at the older man.

"Oh. I'm sorry," said Elric. "That was out of place."

"Yeah, it was," said Shawn. "But you're right. He is an ass." He shoved the last of the bruschetta in his mouth and told his mom he needed to go get his bags. "My ride will be here soon."

"Okay, Shawn, and are you sure you're okay with me not driving you to the airport?" She had told him that tonight was the final dress rehearsal (she had actually said *un-dress* rehearsal) for the shoot they were doing.

The thought made him groan again. "I promise. I'm fine." He looked around the table, then leaned in and whispered into his mother's ear. "Umm, you sure you're going to be okay here? I mean, do you need some protection?"

Torie was shocked. "Shawn! What do you think we're going to do? It isn't that kind of a movie!"

He immediately turned red, averting his eyes. "Mom! I meant like some mace or something."

They stared at one another before breaking out in laughter.

"I'm fine," assured Torie.

Just then, Shawn's phone buzzed, and the text message stated that his ride was turning into the drive. He jumped up, ran up the stairs to grab his bag and met his mother at the door. She gave him a bear hug and a kiss on the cheek. He smiled, waving to everyone else in the house before going outside and jumping into the car.

Torie sighed, watching him pull away. She wouldn't cry because she knew that she was doing the right thing by making him leave. Whatever was going on in this town would require her full attention. She couldn't do that if she had to worry about him.

Returning to the kitchen, she gave everyone her bravest smile.

"You okay?" said Fionna, patting her hand.

"No. But I will be. Okay, so let's get going. The sooner we head out to Trinity Cove, the quicker we get back."

"Sure thing," Jasmin said. "But first we need a couple of items. Follow me."

She led Torie into her mother's study, the small bedroom she had converted to a reading space that sat at the back of the house. There were floor-to-ceiling bookcases that ran the length of one wall, and each was stuffed with books, sitting with their binders out.

Torie walked slowly along the wall, admiring her mother's collection. There were Nicholas Sparks novels, books by Nora Roberts and her alter ego, J.D. Robb. But the most surprising collection seemed to be the entire collected works of Jackie Collins. Torie smiled; her mother continued to surprise her.

Thinking about Alva brought on a wave of sadness. She wanted to reach out to her, call to her. But she knew that seeing her right now would serve to distract her from the job at hand. She needed to know who had killed Alva, Ellie and the other shifters; and seeing the ghost of her mother would have taken her too far out of her headspace to concentrate.

She turned to see Jasmin rifling through the desk that sat near the center of the room. Behind that was a comfortable wing-backed chair with a plaid quilt draped over it.

"What are you looking for?" asked Torie.

"Your son was right. We do need protection. You more than me." She pulled out a necklace made of silver shells, with a turquoise pendant in the shape of a palm hanging from it. She stared at it, then held it up to her ear, almost as if it were whispering an extremely intimate secret. Then she walked over to Torie and offered her the necklace. "Here, wear this?"

"What is it?" asked Torie, regarding the necklace with suspicion.

"It's a necklace. What does it look like?"

"I can see that. But...did it just talk to you?"

"In a manner of speaking," said Jasmin. "It's a blood Hamsa. It's for protection. Normally, a witch would make her own, but since we don't have time for that right now, this will have to do. The fact that it was made by a witch whose blood flows through your veins should allow it to work with you."

Torie took the necklace and slipped it over her head. Instantly, she felt at ease wearing it. "How do I activate it?"

"Let's pray you don't have to. There is no activation to it...it's a ward, a spell that protects at all times. Hopefully it will be strong enough."

"Strong enough for what?"

Jasmin sighed, offering her friend a weak smile. "There are forces in Trinity that are beyond your imagination. Where we are going it's not bad...but you never know. Keep the Hamsa outside your shirt and in plain view at all times."

Torie had more questions but sensed that this was not the time to ask. Instead, she fell into step behind Jasmin as they marched back to the kitchen.

Max turned at their approach and immediately flinched when he saw the necklace Torie was wearing. To her it looked like he had been physically struck.

"Sorry," he said. "That thing packs a punch."

Elric turned to look at it, moving his gaze from the piece of jewelry to Torie's face, and then to Jasmin. He shrugged and turned back to the sink where he had been doing dishes.

"Hey, don't do that," said Torie walking over to him. "I'll get those."

"You most certainly will not," he said. "You cooked this fine meal that I enjoyed. Cleaning up after is my small way of saying thank you."

Max guffawed before Torie could answer. "Let him clean. He likes that stuff."

Torie ignored him but saw the red creep into Elric's cheeks at the words.

"Where is everyone else?" asked Torie, changing the subject.

"Fionna and Glen are back there checking on Eddie, Taylor slipped outside for a moment," said Elric, returning his attention to the sheet pan he was scrubbing.

"You sure we should be splitting up?" Torie questioned.

Jasmin nodded. "There's no other way. Time is crucial, especially if we are facing some kind of rogue witch."

Just then, Fionna and Glen walked back into the kitchen.

"Eddie seems to be getting better," said Fionna. "He's still sedated, but Glen feels that he should be awake fairly soon."

"Shifters really do heal faster than humans," added Glen.

"Do you think he'll be up for some questions when he wakes?" Jasmin asked.

"No way of knowing that. But he's definitely doing much better."

Jasmin's brows creased as she thought. "Torie, you're going to have to go to Trinity without me. I need to stay here to speak with Eddie as soon as he wakes up."

"What? No. This was all your idea," Torie protested.

"Yes, and you'll be fine. Elric will be with you. He knows where to go, and he knows that town a hell of a lot better than I do. You'll be fine. Speak with the veterinarian that Ellie visited; find out what she might know. Then, swing by the hospital and see what you can find out."

"But I've never done anything like this before," Torie said worriedly.

"And you think I have? We're figuring this out as we go." Jasmin paused. "As for you, Fionna, you stay here with me and Eddie. Glen and Max can handle the snooping at the hospital here."

"What about me?" said Taylor.

"Oh, she can come with us," said Max quickly. "Never know when we might need an extra...nose, to sniff things out."

"Gross," said Taylor.

"Or she can stay here as well," said Jasmin, ignoring the wolf. "If whoever is behind this knows that Eddie is still alive, they may try again. We could use an extra set of fangs for protection."

Taylor's face lit up. Given the choice between potentially facing a serial killer and sitting in a car with a werewolf...well, there really wasn't a choice.

"Okay, time to go," said Glen. "Right after shift change is the best time to go snooping around in a hospital. If we're going to do this, we have a small window that will open up in about forty minutes." She gave Fionna a quick kiss and caressed her cheek before walking out the door, wolf in tow.

"Guess that's our cue as well," said Torie, turning to Elric. "I'll drive, you navigate."

They said their goodbyes and headed out of the house to the car. Torie gave one last look over her shoulder at Jasmin and gave her a wave.

"She'll be okay," said Elric. "Witches are not easy to kill." He immediately snapped his head around, giving Torie a horrified look. "I am so sorry. I just have a habit of saying things sometimes before my mind has a chance to edit them."

Torie laughed as she belted herself in. "It's okay, Elric. I've made peace with what happened. Also, it helps that my mother is still floating around in the house somewhere."

"Ugh. I don't know if I'll ever get comfortable with that," Elric said. "Not that I need to be, I mean. I'm sure as soon as this is all solved, we probably won't have to see each other again."

That seemed a little harsh, and Torie told him so.

"I just meant...you won't have to deal with a couple of wolves hanging around your door anymore."

"Oh," she replied. "So, what will the two of you do?"

"No idea. That will be up to Max I guess."

"But you said you were tired of running. Aren't you looking for a place to...I don't know, belong?"

"That would be nice. Somewhere that we aren't constantly feared or hunted or recruited for something."

Torie didn't say anything as she pointed the car in the direction of the highway that would take them south to Trinity Cove.

"So why does it depend on what Max wants? Is it because he's your alpha?"

Elric squirmed a little in his seat. "Yes. Among wolves, there is a strict hierarchy. Alpha's are the first among a pack. Betas follow...and are subservient to the alphas; always. It's true in nature and even more so among werewolves."

"I'm sorry to be asking you all of this," said Torie. "Believe it or not, a week ago I didn't even believe in any of this. So forgive me if I have questions."

"Oh, you can ask me anything," said Elric. "But if I say something that offends you, just know I didn't mean it."

Torie thought about this and decided to press on. "Okay then. How old are you? I mean, do you age like vampires?"

"No. Vampires are long lived. So are we, but not to that degree. I'm forty-eight years old."

Torie would not have guessed that. Yes, he had streaks of gray through his hair and there were definitely some wrinkles crowding the corners of his eyes, but she wouldn't have put his age as being a few years ahead of her.

"And you?" asked Elric, "how old are you?"

"Okay, see, right there; that's one of those things you don't ask a woman." She meant it as a joke, but upon seeing Elric's reaction, she regretted having said it. "Just teasing. It's okay. I'm forty-five. Just had a birthday last month."

"Oh, well happy belated birthday. Was it fun?"

What an odd way to put that, she thought. But it did make her think back, and it also made her realize that no, it wasn't.

She shook her head. "I've had better. My husband—or ex, Jesus I don't even know what to call him anymore—got me a new set of appliances for the kitchen." She gripped the steering wheel tighter, just thinking back to that day.

"You said cooking is important to you," Elric said. "Maybe he thought of it as a way to say thank you."

"Ha. More like a way to say please continue and give me more." She felt the cynicism building and Elric didn't deserve that. What he had just said seemed perfectly logical. "I loved the appliances we had in the house. Ward hated anything that he thought was getting too old. So he would just arbitrarily replace things. Funny that it happened on my last birthday with him. Guess the stove wasn't the only old thing he was tired of."

"But you're so vibrant and full of life," said Elric.

If he hadn't been so sincere, Torie would have laughed. But she could tell he meant every word he had just said, and it caused her to blush.

"So, is it wrong to ask what happened with your husband?"

Awesome. This was just what she wanted to do; repeat that story for the tenth time. But that was exactly what she found herself doing.

Elric listened as she poured her shame out. He didn't interrupt, didn't fidget around; he just listened. And that was exactly what Torie needed at that point.

"And honestly it's not just everything he did. It's the way I got used to feeling around him; things that, looking back, I know were wrong, but seemed so normal at the time. And as my body changed, the worse it became."

"What do you mean your body changed?" Elric asked.

She hadn't expected him to ask for details, but for some reason she felt comfortable enough to proceed. "Honestly, the fatigue is bad. So is the...tenderness in certain parts of my body. My mood swings catch even me by surprise, and my cycle is off. I just feel broken on the inside."

She stopped talking, waiting for him to break the awkward silence.

"Well?" she said, "go ahead and tell me."

"Tell you what?"

"Tell me what I need to do to fix all of that."

Elric turned his head so that he was looking directly at her. "That isn't my place to tell you what to do with your body. I can't fix you, especially when you're not broken. But I can listen and give you what you ask for. I'm sorry. When I said he was an ass earlier, I had no idea just how big of one he was."

"Is," she said. "He's not past tense...at least, I don't think he is." That led to a whirlwind of questions in her mind. What if he was dead? Would she mourn him the way she had her mother? What would she say to Shawn?

"Shawn's a grown man, even though you don't see it," said Elric. "He would be upset of course, but he would process."

Torie took her eyes off the road just long enough to give Elric an incredulous glance.

"Did...how did you know what I was thinking?"

Elric's brow crinkled as he considered her words. "I don't know. Until you mentioned it, I didn't even realize you didn't speak out loud."

She gripped the wheel tighter. *Can you hear me?* she thought.

"Did you hear that?" she asked.

"Hear what?"

"What I just thought? Why were you able to hear me before, but not just then?"

"Well, didn't Jasmin say you can hear the thoughts, or speak to shifters in animal form? Maybe, it works both ways. Maybe you can somehow project your thoughts to shifters."

In a weird sort of way, that made sense. But how did she do it? Was there an on switch that she could toggle?

Elric sensed her discomfort and quickly went back to asking her questions. Aloud.

"So, what other kinds of magic can you do?"

"I don't know. I haven't exactly had time to learn how my powers work. I only just found out."

"The chanting thing is cool. The way Jasmin cast that spell earlier. You'll be able to do that, right?"

"I guess so. Although I do wonder where the rhyming chant came from. I mean, is there some big book of spells that we all have to memorize?"

"I don't think it works like that," Elric said. "From what I know about witchcraft, the uttering of the spell is just to focus the witch's intent. Her intent is what drives the magic."

Torie stole another quick glance. "You seem to know an awful lot about magic."

He shrugged. "Not really. Magic is magic. All supernaturals have a sense for it, but only witches, and maybe certain elf folk, can actually tap into it."

"So, can you sense it with me?"

Elric smiled. "Very much so. It's all around you, waiting for your call." He cleared his throat and pointed to an exit. "We want to take this one. It will take us into town the back way. We can stop by the vet's office first."

Torie was uncomfortable and found herself looking more and more into the side-view mirror to make sure nothing was following them in the darkness.

"So, I have this pendant thing that Jasmin gave me for protection, but should I be worried? Is this town as rough as she says?"

"Nah, it's actually pretty cool; as long as you remember the golden rule. Do unto others before they get a chance to do unto you first."

Torie wasn't sure how she felt about that, and it did nothing to ease her anxiety.

"Head's up, here we go."

Not that she would have needed him to tell her they were entering uncharted territories. One minute she was driving along in the bright, North Carolina sun, and the next, her car was piercing a bubble of blackness. She turned on her headlights and reduced her speed as her eyes adjusted.

"Wait, I thought Jasmin was speaking metaphorically when she said it was a town of perpetual darkness. She meant it literally?"

"Yep. The vampires started a war with the shifter clans here. They intended to create this supernatural darkness all over the world, allowing the vampires to roam freely any time they wanted. They were stopped by a very powerful witch, and she created this forbidden zone that blankets the town. It's like Singing Falls...but bloodier and scarier."

He directed her down a couple of side streets until they pulled up to an unassuming, two-story house. It was one of those homes that doubled as a residential office on the bottom floor and a living residence on the second. Just as they pulled up, the headlights played across the side entrance, just in time to catch a shadowy figure leap out the door and run down the side alley away from the building. Torie thought they were carrying a package under one arm, but it happened so fast she couldn't be sure.

Elric was out of the car in a flash. "Check on Isla...she's the vet here. I'm going after whoever that was!"

And just like that, he shifted into his wolf form and sprinted after the figure at full speed. Torie eyed the broken entrance into the dark building. Grasping her necklace and taking a deep breath, she took a tentative step inside.

# 19

The sudden rush of adrenaline made every nerve in Torie's body hum with energy. She gripped her pendant tightly as she stepped through. The door and the wooden frame it rested in were splintered outward. Whoever had knocked it down was strong. She thought for a moment that maybe she should go back to the car and wait for Elric, but then she remembered he had said the name of the veterinarian.

*Isla.*

What if Isla were in here and injured? Or worse.

She wouldn't leave her. She pressed on, following along a hallway that was only lit by the outside street lamps shining through the small windows along the corridor. She could make out openings to her left in front of her. They looked like mouths yawning, inviting her to enter.

She took a deep breath to steady her trip-hammering heart and peered inside the first opening. It was a large room in which she could just make out cages of various sizes. This had to be where they housed the animals that needed to stay overnight. She breathed a sigh of relief when she realized they were all empty.

She was about to peek into the next room when she heard a noise coming from directly ahead of her. The hallway seemed to end in a large room that she assumed would be the main entrance and lobby of the clinic. Something was shuffling around in there; she could make out paper being shuffled and drawers being opened and closed.

Oh God...what if the intruder wasn't alone? Their partner could still be inside the clinic. She reached into her jeans pocket for her phone. Does a hellmouth have 9-1-1? Then she cursed herself. In her haste to exit the car, she had left her phone in the center console. She kept it there out of habit when she drove.

Why hadn't she listened to Shawn? What she wouldn't give for some mace or pepper spray right now. *Was mace even legal anymore?* she found herself wondering.

*Christ! Snap out of it,* she berated herself as she tried to concentrate on whatever the hell was rifling through the veterinarian's office in a town filled with demons and God knew what else.

Holding her necklace for protection, she remembered what Elric had said about magic and intent. She didn't have any rhyming incantation, but her intent was to not get killed, and she focused on that. Taking a deep breath, she peered into the space the hallway emptied into. It was the back of the receptionist area, and just on the other side of the counter, Torie could make out a form moving around in the darkness.

She took a deep breath and jumped into the space.

"Don't move!" she screamed at the figure, who, cloaked in shadows, raised up from looking through a desk, saw Torie, and screamed.

The scream elicited one from Torie as well.

"Get back!" Torie screamed with as much force as she could muster. She felt something...some force that she never knew dwelt within her, respond to her command.

The shadowy figure was flung backwards, up and over the desk and into the lobby by the energy that flowed from Torie. The thud of the body hitting the chair was accompanied by a female scream. Torie approached the figure carefully, hands in front of her.

"Who are you?" she said, her voice shaky but strong.

"Who am I? I own this place...who are you?" came the pained response as the woman tried to steady herself and rise to her feet.

"Oh...oh my. Are you the veterinarian?" said Torie, reaching to help her stand.

The woman yanked her arm out of Torie's grasp. "Who are you and why are you robbing me?"

"Oh no, I'm not trying to rob anyone. I just pulled up and saw someone in black running out of here. I came in and saw you rummaging around and thought that you were part of whatever was going on."

The woman rubbed the back of her head. "No. I live upstairs, heard what sounded like someone breaking in down here. I came down to see what was going on and was hit over the head. I must have blacked out for a moment because when I came to, I was feeling a little dizzy and trying to brace myself on the desk. That's when you...did whatever you did. What exactly did you do to me?"

Torie looked at her hands. "Honestly, I don't know. My name is Torie. I'm here from Singing Falls."

"Isla Garner," the lady replied. "This is my office." She moved slowly over to the wall near the door and slid her hand along a panel of light switches to illuminate the office space.

Turning back to face Torie, she shrieked, one hand going to her mouth as a large black and silver wolf approached Torie from behind. She pointed, eyes wide, too terrified to scream again.

Torie turned just as Elric shifted back to human to stand next to her.

"Did you catch whoever did this?"

"No. Whoever they were, they were fast. Very fast. I chased them to the outskirts of town, but every time I would get close, they would just speed up. But I caught their scent...definitely the same magic smell from whoever hurt Eddie."

Torie turned to face Isla. "It's okay. This is Elric. He's a friend of mine."

"Nice to meet you in person, Dr. Garner," said Elric, extending a hand.

"You're a werewolf," said Isla, tentatively reaching to shake his hand. "And you're naked."

"We really need to start keeping a change of clothing around if you're going to be doing this a lot," said Torie.

Isla excused herself, went into one of the back exam rooms, and brought back a cloth gown for Elric.

"Not very fashionable, but it will have to do for now. So, the person who broke in, you saw them? But they got away?"

Elric nodded. "Whoever, *what*ever they were, all I could smell was magic cloaking them. But it didn't smell natural; kind of like the way humans spray perfume on themselves to mask their normal body odor. But in this case, the magic masked everything about them."

"Are you okay?" queried Torie, noticing how unsteady the vet looked on her feet.

Isla sat on the desk, rubbing her shoulder. "I will be. Believe it or not, I've had worse." She declined Torie's offer to look at the back of her head. Instead, she patted at it, looked at her palm, and decided the damage wasn't too bad if there was no blood.

"Wait," said Isla, "why are you here? A witch, I am assuming, with a werewolf for a travel companion?"

"Do you know Ellie Shielding? She is...*was*...our vet in Singing Falls," said Torie.

Isla perked up instantly. "Yes, I know her. And what do you mean 'was'?"

"She's dead," said Torie. "We believe she was killed by the same murderer who's been killing shifters."

Even in the harsh fluorescent office lighting, Isla went pale.

"I told her to be careful, to not get involved in paranormal issues."

"We know she was here. She brought you a blood sample to analyze. Is there anything you can tell us that might help?"

"Well, I did analyze the sample and called her with the results. I still have a copy of what was found." She moved to a large four-drawer file cabinet that took up much of the back wall. She stopped short as she realized it had been broken open. Pulling out a drawer second from the top, she searched through it quickly before turning to face Torie and Elric.

"It's gone," she said. "The report and the blood sample." She turned and beckoned them to follow her down the hall to her private office. "I kept a copy of it on my computer also."

She flicked on the screen, only to be greeted with a blank, blue monitor. Looking to the left, she sighed, pinching the bridge of her nose between her thumb and forefinger.

"The tower is gone. Someone swiped my whole computer," she said in exasperation.

"That must have been what the thief was carrying," said Elric.

Isla turned to him. "So someone, or something, was able to outrun a werewolf while carrying an old-school computer tower? I don't know of anything capable of that...except maybe a cheetah shifter."

"No," said Elric. "I can't explain it...it didn't move like a shifter. It was too comfortable on two legs. It sounds weird, I know; it's hard to explain."

"Well, I don't have the report, but I can tell you the report found some very interesting compounds that I haven't come across before. There was a large dose of Myosotis and Solanaceae, more commonly known as forget-me-not and nightshade. There were also lesser amounts of various mushrooms and something that couldn't be identified."

"All of that was in the blood sample she gave you? I don't even know what any of those are."

"Well, I can only tell you what was found, the rest is up to you. But if it helps, when I told Ellie, she seemed to have an 'ah-ha' moment. She was very excited and thanked me."

Torie grabbed a pencil and piece of paper from Isla's desk and wrote out the names of everything she had found in the blood sample. She held the paper up to Elric.

"Maybe this is what the killer didn't want us to know. Ellie obviously knew what this meant. Again, this just confirms there is a supernatural killer?"

"And we do what with this information?" asked Elric.

"We hope that Jasmin will know."

Elric smiled as understanding flooded him.

*Don't say anything,* thought Torie, hoping the wolf would hear her. *This vet seems like she's a good person, but we don't know who we can and can't trust yet.*

Elric smiled and nodded again. Good. She was getting better at this magic communication thing.

"Is there somewhere you can go, someone we can call?" said Torie, looking at Isla.

"Oh, I'll be fine. I just need to clean up this place. My wife will be home soon. She's used to dealing with supernaturals on a more... physical basis. I'll be fine."

As reluctant as Torie was to leave her, she knew that the sooner they got this info back to Jasmin, the closer they would be to solving these murders.

"Thank you," said Torie. She scribbled down her number on another piece of paper and shoved it into Isla's hand. "If you need anything at all; call me."

With that, she and Elric left, heading down the hallway that led to the side entrance and her car.

"Christ that was scary," she said, wringing her hands and waiting for her body to flush the increased adrenaline out of her system.

"You used your witchcraft," said Elric. "I could smell it crackling all around you when I entered the building."

"That was probably the most frightening thing about it," she replied. "I have no idea where it came from."

"Fight or flight," said Elric. "Your body chose fight. Good for you."

They were silent as she eased out of the parking lot and aimed her car at the main street that would take them out of this cursed town. She'd had enough of this dark place and wanted nothing more than to get back home and see the sunlight again. The information they had just received was far more important than anything the hospital might have offered.

"So, you have no idea what that was?" Torie asked.

"Not at all. Of course, that doesn't mean much in a town like this. There are supernaturals here that even I have never heard of."

Torie was shaking her head in disbelief. "Werewolves, witches, vampires...all the things I always thought were just make believe. They really are out there going bump in the night."

"If it's any consolation, I used to believe that humans were made up."

Torie nearly choked as the shock of what he said hit her.

"What are you talking about? Of course we exist."

"Max and I are from the dark dimension that runs parallel to your world. The two dimensions were forever separated by the Forbidding, the great barrier that split my world from that of man. The Forbidding was created long ago, before anyone in my lineage was born. It was reinforced by the witches of this world. They were tasked with keeping our world of darkness at bay.

"Not long ago, a great war erupted between a vampire and his werewolf clan, and the shifters that had become part of your world. A very powerful witch- one that pretty much controls Trinity Cove- created a new race of shifters to join her battle—"

"Wait, a new race of shifters? What do you mean?"

"Well, we are all born into what we are—wolf, tiger, bear, you name it—but this witch, she was a descendant of the witch line that had erected the Forbidding; powerful witches to say the least. So, in an effort to increase her army numbers against the vampire, she cast a spell that created totem shifters. Humans who long held a belief that they are only human on the outside, but their spirit was that of some other being; unicorn, harpy, mermaid...whatever they felt they were internally. Well, the spell that was cast focused on an item these humans carried with them—their totem—and it allowed them to shift into their inner form at will.

"With such a formidable army at her side, she defeated the vampire and in so doing, changed the law of the Forbidding locking the darkness over this town twenty-four seven."

"But why would she allow the darkness here at all?"

"Because with the original containment spell broken, the darkness would have kept spreading, engulfing everything in its path. As powerful as this witch was, she couldn't stop it completely; but she could localize it. To Trinity Cove."

"That's incredible," said Torie. "How come I've never heard this before? For that matter, why isn't it all over the news?"

Elric smiled and gestured. "Magic. The town, while well known to paranormals and the humans that decided to stay here and make it their home, is largely hidden away from the rest of the world."

"And you decided not to stay here? You and Max?"

Elric looked away, studying the view that was taking shape outside of his window as they drove out of the darkness.

"Sometimes, if you decide to dwell for too long in darkness, it becomes all you know. Everything becomes a shadow that you either run from or fight. We knew there had to be more out there, so we headed north; out of the dark and into the light of the mountains." He turned and looked at Torie. "Hopefully, we will find something worth climbing out of the darkness for."

Torie smiled, unsure what to say at that moment. Just then, her phone rang.

"This is Torie…Whoa, hold on…go slow, what are you talking about? Another murder? Oh my god…we're on our way back now."

Elric looked at her as she closed the call. "What is it? Who has been killed?"

Torie gritted her teeth and white-knuckled the steering wheel as they headed back into town.

"It's Max. He's been accused of killing Taylor."

## 20

There was a frenzy in town the likes of which Torie had not seen outside of Black Friday at Nieman Marcus. She drove right to the town police station, a small, unassuming brick building, that looked more like a freestanding restaurant than a police station.

Outside, there was a throng of photographers shouting questions at a couple of officers who were working hard to keep them back from the station doors.

Torie parked the car at the rear of the parking lot then approached the building on foot with Elric in tow. As they approached the reporters, they heard a sharp "Pssst" hissed at them from the corner of the building.

It was Fionna, gesturing for them to come around to where she was standing out of sight of the mass of people. Well, by mass, it was probably a dozen people shouting, but by Singing Falls standards, it might as well have been a couple hundred.

"Fionna," said Elric, "what the hell is going on? Where is Max?"

"He's inside. They have him locked up," she said, her eyes filled with tears, her voice trembling. "They think he killed Taylor."

"Who's they?" Torie asked.

"The police. They kept it quiet, but they called in some special agents and detectives from Trinity who have been working the case. They...they caught Max, with...with..." She burst into tears, unable to continue. Torie grabbed the shifter and pulled her close in a bear hug, rocking her gently.

"They have him locked up?" said Elric. "In a cage? No, he can't take that. Plus, he would never hurt Taylor."

He started to walk past Fionna, heading for a door on the side of the building.

"No," she said, stretching out a hand to grab at his arm. "You can't go in there. They think he had an accomplice and they are looking for you. They know you are both wolves, and right now they have half the town whipped into a blood frenzy. Plus, you're half naked... you need clothes before someone sees you."

Elric looked down at himself, shocked to remember that he was only wearing a hospital gown.

"Fine," he said, shrugging out of the gown and shifting to his canine form in the blink of an eye. He looked up at Torie. *I have to see Max.*

"Okay, that's probably even worse," said Torie. She turned to Fionna. "Where is Jasmin?"

"She's inside talking to the detective from Trinity. Someone named Barnes."

Elric whimpered at the name.

*He's a wolf shifter from Trinity. Corrupt as night is black there. He always had it in for Max because Max is an alpha like him, and he refused to cede any of his territory to Barnes.*

"Elric says there's bad blood between this guy Barnes and Max," she relayed to Fionna. "Says he's a wolf shifter too."

"What? Are you sure? There's no scent coming off him. He smells like the rest of the humans."

Torie looked at Elric. *Could it be the same person that had broken into the vet's office?*

Elric growled in response.

"Look," said Torie, bending down to stare into Elric's yellow eyes. "If there is a possibility of a connection here, you can't go in there. Let me go in. I'll talk to Jasmin and see what's going on. We'll take care of Max, I promise. But you go back to my house and wait there, okay?" She sensed his reluctance; he didn't need to verbalize anything to her. "Please, Elric. It won't do either of you any good if you end up in a cell as well."

Again the wolf growled. Against his better judgment, he turned and loped off in the direction of an open glen behind the station house before sprinting for the woods just on the other side of the clearing.

"So...when did that start?" asked Fionna, wiping at her tears. "The communication between the two of you."

"By-product of our little adventure," she replied. "I'll have to fill you in later. First, we need to get in there and talk to Jasmin. Plus, I need to know what happened to Taylor."

Just as they reached for the door, Torie stopped and looked at Fionna. "I'm sorry about Taylor. I know she was your friend, and I also know what you're feeling right now."

Fionna's eyes were red and swollen, but she still gave Torie a hard stare. "I'm sad and hurt. But most of all I'm pissed off. We're going to get whoever did this. And Goddess help them when we do."

Torie nodded, and together they passed through the door into the station. Voices, some angry and some calling for calm, filled Torie's ears. They made their way through a dimly lit corridor that led to the back of a work area. A young deputy stood with her back to them, trying to calm down a group of men on the other side of the counter she manned.

"I'm sorry, Sir, I know who you are, but no one is authorized back there just yet," she said.

"What's going on? Who is that?" whispered Torie.

"Some hot shot lawyer supposedly. Wants to represent Max. Word's gotten out that this town has a serial killer and they think he's been caught. News and ambulance chasers have come out of the woodworks."

She took Torie by the arm and pulled her around the hall, away from the front desk commotion, and down another corridor that led to a small office. Inside, Torie could make out Jasmin's voice.

"Oh, come on, Dwayne, you know as well as I do that Max didn't kill Taylor."

"I don't know any such thing," came a gruff reply. "Jasmin, you know as well as I do that all of this started when those wolves came to town. As far as we know, this is shifter on shifter violence."

"He was helping us! Why would he do that if he was the killer?" she said just as Torie and Fionna entered the room.

"I have no idea what goes on in the minds of psychopaths. Or wolves in human clothing...besides, there is nothing any of us can do at this point. Those officers from Trinity are like FBI or something. They have claimed jurisdiction of this case. They just went to get a signed order that will let them take Max out of here. Once that happens, maybe this town can get back to normal, and the residents can stop living in fear."

"If they take him, he's as good as dead," Torie said.

"Who are you?" The man was tall and imposing, large of stature with a body that had seen one too many bowls of ice cream after dinner. He had a mustache and just the hint of a beard. He narrowed his eyes and locked them on Torie.

"This is Alva's daughter, she just moved to the area. She's a friend," said Jasmin. "Torie, this is Dwayne. He's the sheriff here. So how do you know Max is as good as dead?"

"I heard that the team that is here to take him back to Trinity is working for an alpha there who has it in for Max. That's why he's here...he's trying to start his life over away from all the craziness down in Trinity Cove."

"Oh?" said the sheriff. "And who told you this?"

Torie started to speak but stopped herself.

"Uh huh. Just what I thought. By any chance would you happen to know where his partner is? The beta that's been running around with him? I've a feeling he hasn't strayed too far from his master."

"Dwayne Arsenio Smith!" scolded Jasmin. "You stop that kind of talk right now. I've certainly had my doubts about these wolves up until now, but I'm telling you they didn't do this."

Torie eyed her friend. She was more than a little shocked to hear Jasmin defending Max and Elric.

"We caught him red-handed."

"What exactly did you see him do?" questioned Torie.

The sheriff scratched his head. "We didn't actually see it, but the evidence can't be ignored."

Jasmin turned to Torie. "He had just returned from...his work with Glen at the hospital," she was careful to give Torie a look that told her not to reveal too much about what they had all been up to, "and he got this weird look on his face, per Glen. He told her something wasn't right, and then shifted to wolf form and went sprinting up the road from where Glen and Fionna live.

"Taylor lives alone in a house just over the hillside from there. Glen knew something was wrong and called us. We got there just as this guy—" she shot a thumb towards Dwayne, "was hauling him out in handcuffs."

"Don't leave out the naked and bloody part," said Dwayne. He eyed Jasmin and then turned to face Torie. "We received a call that someone was screaming and yelling for help, so we dispatched a deputy to Taylor's residence. They heard a howling sound, kicked in the door, and found Max bent over Taylor's body. She had been ripped to shreds and his hands were covered in her blood."

Torie shuddered. She had never liked gory movies, and the fact that she now seemed to find herself front and center in one, made her stomach churn.

"Okay, first of all," said Jasmin, "no one lives within earshot of Taylor's house, so who made the call to you? Has this mysterious person shown up to make a statement? Don't you find it suspicious that the call came just in time for one of your deputies to walk in on this scene? And you know as well as I do that one deputy could not have taken Max if he didn't want to come along peacefully. Plus, you said Max hasn't spoken once after bringing him in. Why is that?

Because he's in shock! He was in love with Taylor...we all knew that. Why would he do this to her?"

"Hell if I know, Jasmin. Maybe for the same reason he did it to all of the other shifters in the area that he's killed."

"You know that isn't true," said Jasmin, crossing her arms and turning her back to him.

Torie nodded. "He knows. Otherwise, why would he tell us so much about a case like this. Something isn't sitting right with him either."

Sheriff Smith didn't say anything, only narrowed his eyes again at Torie.

"What are you?" Torie asked. "I mean, you're obviously a supernatural because you know about everyone. Or are you one of the select few humans that are let in on the secret around here?"

"I'm a dwarf," he said after a slight pause.

Torie arched her eyebrows. "Forgive me, but...I thought dwarfs were...vertically challenged?"

The sheriff looked indignant. "And I always thought all witches had long noses with a wart at the end of them."

"Touché," Torie replied. From now on she was going to keep what she thought she knew about the supernatural to herself. Had everything she had learned from Hollywood been a lie?

"So what now?" asked Jasmin. "You're just going to give Max over to them and then what? Hunt down Elric and do the same?"

"Look, I don't like this anymore than you do," said the sheriff, lowering his voice to a whisper. "But the fact remains, he was caught with Taylor's blood all over him at the scene of the crime. I've got a town filled with terrified people, someone called in the big dogs from Trinity, and now Max won't tell us what happened. My hands are tied."

"Wait," said Torie, "someone called Trinity about this? You didn't ask for their help?"

"Of course not. Those guys creep me out. I'd never call them in."

"What do you want to bet it's the same mysterious caller that alerted you to send a deputy to Taylor's place?"

"Okay, maybe *your* hands are tied, but ours aren't," said Torie. "How long do we have before they come back with that order to take Max?"

"Twenty-four hours," Dwayne replied. "And when they show up, there is nothing I can do at that point."

"Come on then," Torie said to Jasmin.

"Where to?"

"To catch a predator."

"Oh, I used to love watching that...wait, are you thinking what I think you're thinking?"

"Yep. We set up a sting. Now we just need the perfect bait."

"Bait for what?" said Fionna as she stepped into the room. She had refused to stay by their side when the talk had turned to what happened to Taylor.

Torie and Jasmin looked at one another before turning their heads to Fionna.

## 21

"Are you crazy?" asked the sheriff. "There is no way I can condone this."

"Oh hush, Dwayne," said Jasmin. "The less you know the better. Let us handle this; you just look for a way to delay that court order in case we need a little extra time."

He thought for a minute. "Well, the judge does owe me a favor after I landscaped his daughter's wedding venue. You know we dwarfs have a way with stone-work. We—"

Jasmin waved him off, turning to face Fionna. "Listen to me, baby girl... we are going to get the bastard who did this to Taylor. Are you with us?"

Fionna's eyes hardened, her features growing dark. "Whatever you need."

"Good," said Torie. "But it's going to be very dangerous."

"I'm fine with that," Fionna replied. "This has to end. Now."

"Okay, one last thing," said Torie, turning to the sheriff. "I need to get in there and speak to Max."

"Told you, he's not talking."

"He'll talk to me," she said. "Please."

He looked around the office, letting out a deep sigh as he contemplated her request.

"Okay, but make it quick. And if anyone sees you back there..."

"They won't, I promise," Torie said.

"Well, I don't know anything," said the sheriff, turning his back to them. "Max is in the holding cell, third door down on your right. Not my fault if curiosity seekers wander around back there..." With that, he left the room, making his way towards the front of the police station where there was still considerable commotion going on.

"Come on," Torie said, taking Fionna and Jasmin by the hands as they rushed out of the room and towards the back of the building.

Each room they passed was dark and silent, but the third room was dimly lit with a single can light recessed into the ceiling. Inside the room was a single, metal desk with what looked like built-in handcuffs attached to it. Behind the desk was a cell with iron bars and an intimidating padlock securing the door.

Inside, on a single cot suspended from the wall by a set of chains, sat Max. He was cross-legged, his head down, staring at his hands which were clasped in his lap. They were dark brown, and it took Torie a moment to realize they were stained with dried blood.

Taylor's blood.

The bastards hadn't even let him clean up.

"Max," whispered Jasmin, loud enough that she knew he could hear her. He didn't respond and, for a brief moment, Torie wondered if he were still alive.

She sighed relief as he shifted in place, but he still refused to look up at the women.

"Max, are you okay?" Jasmin asked. She walked over to the cell and placed her hands on the bars. "Max, we're here to help you, but you have to talk to us."

Still no response. Jasmin stepped back and glanced at Torie, shrugging her shoulders.

Torie stepped up to the cell, taking Jasmin's place. "Max, we know you didn't do this. We have a lead; Elric and I found something down in Trinity that is going to help prove you didn't do this."

"You found something?" said Jasmin. "Why didn't you lead with that? You could have told me."

Torie gave her an exasperated look, pointing at Max silently with her hand. Jasmin nodded, motioning for her to continue.

Quieting her thoughts as much as she could, Torie reached out with her mind. She had no way of knowing if it would work with him or not. When she had communicated telepathically with Elric it had just happened.

*Max...can you hear me?* she asked silently.

He didn't answer, but she saw a change in his posture; his back stiffened slightly and his head cocked to one side just a little.

*If you can hear me, you have to help us help you. We have a plan, but in order to do it, we need to know what happened with...with Taylor. I'm sorry she is dead. I understand how you felt about her.*

*No,* came his reply. His thoughts were all wolf voice now, deep and guttural as they blasted into her mind. *No, you do not know how I felt about her. You don't know, because I don't understand what I felt. Wolves mate for life...we are fated to other wolves. But for some reason...I felt Taylor on a level that I can't explain.*

His head dropped and his body began to rock slowly; it was obvious he was racked with pain. Torie probed, trying to understand the emotions he, and by extent she, was feeling.

Grief overwhelming everything else. And regret.

*It's okay, Max, I know how you feel. It's hard looking back and thinking about all the small moments where you could have made a change...especially when that change would have had a profound impact on the present. We all have our 'what if' moments. But you can't dwell on that, because I doubt there is any magic in the world that can change the past.*

He looked up, tears streaking his face as his eyes came into focus. He wept openly as he stood and made his way to the bars, placing his hands on Torie's and resting his head against the iron, his forehead touching hers.

Together they cried; he for a love that might have been, her for a love she had let slip away.

"You...you mourn your husband, that he got away from you?" Max said aloud.

Torie shook her head, wiping the tears from her eyes.

"No. My mother. I am mourning the time we should have had." She offered him a weak smile and patted his hand through the bars. "Now. We are going to get the murdering asshole who did this. Are you up for some vengeance?"

His eyes mirrored Fionna's as his whole being filled with a single desire; to tear the killer limb from limb.

"You need to tell us what happened," said Torie. "There might be something in the details that could help us."

He took a deep breath, forcing his mind to retread painful memories.

"I was with Glen. We had just returned to her house from the hospital. Everything there checked out, so we knew that was a dead end. Suddenly, I had this feeling...I can't really explain it. I'm an alpha and I have a sense for when anyone in my pack is in danger. It's an empathic bond that we all share. But this time, it wasn't Elric that I sensed; it was Taylor.

"I can't explain why or how, but I knew she was in danger. I think I am...*was*...fated to be with her. And though she fought it, she felt it too." He looked at Fionna, his eyes soft and sorrowful. She only nodded; admitting what the wolf sensed and had never acknowledged.

"I knew that whatever was happening to her, it had to be life-threatening for it to ring out to me like that. I don't even remember shifting to my wolf form; one minute I was standing there talking to Glen, and the next I was a mile away, racing through the fields.

"I had never been to Taylor's house, but I was drawn to her. I knew the farmhouse in the distance was where she was, and I could feel her screaming out to me. I leapt through the window, crashing into the house just as a figure dressed in black stood up. He had been hunched over Taylor...doing something to her.

"I saw red as I gave myself over to my wolf completely. I lost all sense of self as I charged him. I jumped, landing on him and shifting into my hybrid form. I think, for some reason, a part of me thought I would have a better chance against him if I had hands as well as fangs.

"I was wrong. He...it...whatever, was so strong and fast. It caught me in mid-air, like I was nothing. One hand around my throat, then, moving faster than I could follow, it hit me. I saw stars, maybe even blacked out for a second. The next thing I know, I woke up lying next to Taylor."

He stopped to gather himself, swallowing hard. "She was bleeding out. Her throat had been slashed, her body...looked like..." He couldn't finish, and all of the women in the room were thankful for that. "Anyway, I picked up her body, cradling it...I just wanted to hold her, that was all. That's when I heard the front door smash in and the officer came in, gun drawn, telling me not to move.

"So I didn't. I didn't move."

"That description sounds a lot like the same character we caught at the vet's office in Trinity," said Torie. "But how could it have gotten from Trinity to Singing Falls so quickly?"

"Whatever it was, it reeked of magic," said Max. "It was fast...way faster than me or any shifter I've ever come across."

"So how do we lure it into the open?" asked Fionna.

"I think the bigger question is why is it attacking again? Why Taylor?" implored Jasmin.

Torie's eyes lit up. "We're getting too close to it for comfort." She dug into her pocket and fished out the piece of paper she had carried from Isla Garner's office and handed it over to Jasmin. "This thing killed Ellie because she knew something. Whatever this is was a clue I believe."

Jasmin studied it intently. "You got this from the vet?"

"Yes. It's the same information that Ellie had and was bringing to you the day she was killed. Do you know what it is?"

"I just might," she replied. "We need to get to your mother's house."

"What? Why there?" asked Torie.

"Your mother was the most talented potion maker I ever met," said Jasmin. "You name it, she could make a potion for it. I'm betting she has these ingredients at her workshop. If I can get them, see what exactly they can be combined for, it might tell us even more about the killer."

"But what does any of this have to do with Taylor?" questioned Fionna.

Torie took her hand. "Nothing. If we are getting close, then this thing is trying to take some of the heat off itself." She turned and looked at Max. "By framing him."

"You can't go after this thing alone," said Max. "There's no way you're a match for it."

"Well, we still have Elric on our side," said Jasmin.

The mention of his beta made Max even more uneasy. "No. I've already lost one person I care about today. I won't allow it to happen to another."

"Well, you're stuck in here for the time being, so there isn't much else we can do," said Torie.

Max arched an eyebrow at her before placing his hands on the bars again. He groaned, his muscles tightening as he slowly began to spread the bars apart until there was an opening big enough for him to step through.

"Wow," said Torie. "You're a lot stronger than you look."

"You better get your skinny ass back in that cell!" said Jasmin.

"But he can help us," said Torie.

"Bitch, I am not going to jail for no wolf. We were the last ones back here with him, there is no way they won't pin his escape on us. Besides, if we take him with us, they'll know where to come looking for him. We can't help anyone with that kind of heat."

As much as she hated to admit it, Torie knew leaving Max in jail was the best option for the moment. She reached out with her mind and told him to stay put for now. She also promised that she would do everything in her very limited power to protect Elric. She didn't want to see anyone else in this town get hurt, especially not someone she was just getting to know and like.

Max sensed that last sentiment and gave her a questioning look.

In return, her cheeks flamed crimson and she turned away as he stepped back into his cell and bent the bars back into place.

"What was that about?" queried Jasmin.

"What?" said Torie, playing dumb in a too obvious kind of way.

"Well, we have a lot to talk about it seems. But not now. First, we have a trap to set."

"Yes," replied Torie, "and I think I know just how to do it."

"Hey," said Max. "I have one last thing that might be of help to you."

"Oh, what's that?" said Torie.

"I bit the bastard."

Jasmin's eyes widened as she began to rummage around through her purse. She found a small vial that contained a perfume sample from the local Bath and Beauty shop. She quickly emptied it out and handed the vial to Max.

He began to shift, but just enough that he was still mostly human, only his head and jawline turned more bestial as he took the vial and brought it to his mouth. He retched hard as a dark liquid spilled from his mouth into the vial. Shifting back to his human form, he handed it to Jasmin.

"Blood sample," he said. "Maybe you can use it to help track him down."

"Well that's just all kinds of nasty," said Jasmin, placing the vial back in her bag and shaking her head.

## 22

Lights flashed in Fionna's face and she blinked rapidly, trying to keep them from blinding her.

The assemblage of press was more than Torie had imagined it would be, but the story of a crazed serial killer on the loose in a small, bucolic town was starting to gather national attention. They all clamored, calling out to Fionna who stood in front of the porch of Torie's mother's house.

"Be sure to stand far enough away from the house that the cameras can catch enough detail to identify the location of the home," Torie had told her. "We want the killer to see where we are."

The thought of that seemed to run opposite to what Fionna's instinct told her. As much as she wanted vengeance, she didn't relish the thought of putting herself in such a vulnerable position.

With Jasmin at her side, she put on a brave face for the cameras.

Raising her hands, Jasmin implored the crowd to quieten. "Ladies and gentlemen, thank you for coming over like this. As some of you who live in this town may know, we are all saddened by the senseless killing of one of our own. As you also know, this isn't the first time, or even the second, that this has happed. This is Fionna Gate. She is the best friend of the latest victim, and she has something to say."

Fionna cleared her throat and stepped up. "I am here to say that, while I am grateful to the Singing Falls Police Department for attempting to bring Taylor's killer to justice; I want them and everyone listening to know this: they have the wrong man in custody."

There was a murmur that passed through the crowd, followed by more camera flashes and a barrage of questions.

Again, Jasmin held up her hands before motioning for Fionna to continue.

"You are probably wondering how I know this. Well, I have proof of what I am saying. The killer left behind a piece of evidence that I collected from Taylor's house. It aligns with more evidence we were able to get from a source in Trinity Cove. I have already called the federal authorities about this. Not the branch in Trinity, mind you. They will be here tomorrow to discuss the matter, and I can assure you justice will be served."

With that, she turned and went back into the house, careful to give the press one last coy look over her shoulder as she shut the door, leaving Jasmin to deal with the throng of hungry reporters demanding to know more.

"Holy crap," she said to Torie, letting out a deep breath. "That was scary."

"Well, it looks like you certainly kicked a hornets' nest," said Jasmin as she came inside, hurriedly closing the door after. She took her phone out of her pocket and smiled as she flicked it to life, raising it to her ear. "Well hello, Dwayne Arsenio Smith. That didn't take long."

She brought the phone away from her ear and rolled her eyes as the sheriff's voice carried throughout the living room.

"Look, it's okay...no, of course there are no federal authorities coming...yes I know that...it had to be done...I am sorry for how this makes your department look, but in all honesty, if you were doing a better job at catching this killer, we wouldn't have had to take things into our own hands."

With that, she flicked at the screen with her thumb, disconnecting the call.

"Man, I really miss my flip phone at times like this. There was nothing like the feel of snapping it shut on A-holes like that."

"So I did okay?" asked Fionna.

"Girl, you did an amazing job," said Jasmin. "If I was a killer, I'd be on my way over right now to cut your ass."

That elicited a round of nervous groans from everyone.

"Don't worry," said Elric, "it won't come to that. Whatever is doing this will not get close enough to hurt you. I promise." His eyes flashed yellow for a split second. That, added to the tone in his voice, sent shivers up Torie's spine.

"Okay, we have to act fast. We only have a few hours before sundown and I'm betting the killer will strike then."

"But what if he or she knows it's a trap?" worried Fionna.

"Already covered that," said Torie, nodding in Jasmin's direction.

"Yes," said Jasmin, "one of the reporters out there is not only a community member but also a friend of the family, if you will. She's a deer shifter and is just as anxious as we are to see this ended. She's going to 'leak' a story that you're staying here with Torie tonight, and that according to rumors, the local PD is so angry with you for not turning over any evidence you have, they are refusing to provide you protection."

"Sounds forced," said Torie, "do you think it will work?"

"I'm betting it will. The killer is becoming frantic. Why else would they risk attacking Taylor in broad daylight just to frame a werewolf? They have to know that Ellie was coming here to tell your mother what she knew...all of this should be too much for them to resist. They'll definitely show up at some point."

"And when they do," said Elric, "They're going down."

Torie took a deep breath. "Okay, before we get too cocky, let's remember that whatever this thing is, it was faster than you, and stronger than Max."

Elric only stared at her, then made his way into the kitchen alone.

Fionna started after him, only to be stopped by Torie.

"I got it," she said, following after the wolf.

He was standing, hands clasped behind his back as he looked out one of the windows.

"Hey, what's going on, Elric? Talk to me."

"I hate this," he said, not turning to face her. "I feel so weak and inept."

Torie nodded, wishing she could take back the words she had said in the living room. "And in your mind, I just confirmed that you are less than whatever it is we are facing. I'm sorry for that."

"Don't be," he replied. "I know you didn't mean it the way that I took it; but you have to realize, all my life I've only followed. I never lead. That is the life of a beta. I hate my station; always seen as less than. Not an equal to Max and now not an equal to a supernatural killer either."

Torie thought for a moment, an idea flashing through her mind.

"Elric, what exactly is it that binds you to Max? Why can't you be your own man? Have you ever thought about just starting your own life?"

This time he turned to face her, a weary smile barely crossing his features. "If only it were that easy. But you were right when you said we are bound together. The bond between wolves, especially the one that governs alpha and beta, runs deep. It is mystical in nature."

"Well, then maybe it's a good thing that you're surrounded by witches. If it was created by magic, maybe the bond can be severed by magic. If that's what you want."

He stared at her, unsure what to say.

"I've never been offered a choice in anything," he said. "I truly don't know how to respond to that. Even if it were possible...what would I be?"

"More than what you are now." She moved closer to him. "And who's to say you'd have to go through it alone? There's a whole community here built on mutual support. You said you and Max were looking for a place to belong; maybe this is it."

"Sorry to interrupt," said Jasmin, walking quickly into the room and giving Torie a biting glance, "but I need to get busy working on figuring out what these ingredients you discovered create. And I'll need your help." She passed by them, heading into the workspace at a fast clip.

"Um, sure," said Torie, glancing at Elric as she headed for the backroom. "Can we finish this talk later?"

He nodded, watching as she went to join Jasmin.

"Where is Eddie?" Torie asked, feeling guilty that she was just now realizing the cat shifter was gone.

"They took him to Glen's house earlier today. She can keep a much closer eye on him there and she has everything needed to help him mend," said Jasmin. "Plus, he's still in no shape to help us, and we can't risk him getting hurt more than he already has been. Shifters are tough, but they have their limits."

"So, we're going to make a potion?" said Torie. "Is that something I may have inherited from my mother?"

At the mention of her mother, Alva appeared, translucent and glowing. She smiled at her daughter.

"You called?" she said.

"Um, no, and I will never get used to that," said Torie. She smiled back at her mother, happy to see her after the adventures she had been through recently.

"Well, maybe you didn't call, but we can use her help," said Jasmin, as she looked around the workshop. "Alva, where do you keep all of your potion-making ingredients?"

Alva pointed to a large curio that hulked in the far corner of the space.

Jasmin opened the door to reveal empty shelves. She frowned, looking at the ectoplasmic form. "There's nothing in here."

"There most certainly is," said Alva. "You just can't see it. Everything is protected by a cloaking spell."

"Oh, that's just great," said Jasmin. "Can you undo it for us?"

"I wish I could, my friend, but for some reason I can't work magic in this form."

"Well, can't *you* undo the spell?" asked Torie, looking to Jasmin.

"No. Only the spell-caster can recall it." Jasmin thought for a moment, then glanced Torie's way, a sly grin spreading across her face.

"What is it?"

"I can't break the spell, but maybe *you* can. You share your mother's bloodline, so maybe the spell will respond to you."

"Oh, that's an excellent idea," said Alva. "Certainly worth a try."

"Alva, can you tell us the incantation you would have used?"

Alva thought hard before shaking her head. "I can't remember."

"That's okay, it may not be necessary. It just would have been nice to know some of the trigger words to give Torie something to work with." She turned to Torie and fixed her with a gaze. "The thing to remember about spells is that they are the embodiment of the caster's will."

"Yes, I know. Elric explained that to me."

Jasmin frowned. "Once we get through all of this, you and I are going to have a very serious conversation about...the supernatural order of things. But for now, this cloaking spell was created with the intent to hide everything behind it; to keep it from prying eyes. What you need to do, is fix your mind on undoing that. First, close your eyes, and just reach out with your hand...reach into the cabinet and tell me what you feel."

Torie stepped forward and did as she was told. Her hand stopped as soon as she put it in the cabinet.

"It feels like there's a wall here, a spongy one that I can't get past."

"Okay that's good," said Jasmin. "I myself can reach fully into the cabinet and feel nothing. That means you're sensitive to your mother's spells. This is a good thing."

Torie opened her eyes, withdrawing her hand. "So what do I do?"

"Well, you're going to have to break the spell. You need to fix your intent on what you want to happen—in this case, revealing the contents of the shelves—and then make it happen. Trust the magic inside of you to do the heavy lifting."

Torie thought back to the feeling of striking out at Isla Garner with the force in her mind. She had no idea how she did that, but it seemed to have come from the strong emotion—namely fear—that she was feeling at the time. She wasn't afraid here, but she knew that she had to draw on something other than just her desire for the objects to appear.

She had an idea. Extending both hands until she again felt resistance, she took a deep, calming breath and pictured the wall before her vanishing. Then, eyes closed, she whispered:

> "Worlds near and far, and those in between,
> reveal to me now, that which can't be seen."

Opening her eyes, she saw the cabinet was no longer empty. Instead it was filled with small mason jars filled with herbs and powders. There was also an entire shelf that had nails driven into the edge. From each nail hung a different dried herb, each with the name of it written on a piece of tape on the shelf above. She smiled, her hand floating to her chest.

"I don't believe it. It worked," she said to Jasmin.

Jasmin gave her an appreciative nod. "Look at you, getting all witchy with it. But don't get cocky...and a piece of advice. Careful calling on the powers of other worlds; you never know who or what might be listening."

That was a sobering thought, and Torie filed it away, determined to do better next time. Provided there would be a next time.

The ghost of her mother was all smiles and began to clap soundlessly.

"Well done, daughter! I knew you had it in you."

Torie took the compliment in stride as she watched Jasmin go about pulling down jar after jar from the cabinet and then a few of the hanging herbs as well. She carried them to the large worktable and sat them down, studying the ingredients.

"Do you know what to make with them?" asked Torie.

"I have a feeling," she replied, absentmindedly. "Potions are just like cooking. Once you know what the ingredients are, you know how to put them together; what can't overpower what. This for instance —" she pointed to a jar with a gray powder in it— "is Ragweed. It can only be combined with this one—" she picked up another jar filled with a white powder— "in very small amounts. The two together can be a horrendous poison. But if you mix them with the ground-up leaves of a poinsettia, and add the right incantation, it becomes a love potion."

She studied the ingredients, muttering to herself. "The trick is to figure out what everything on that list can make when combined properly, and then decide which one is most likely the potion used by our killer."

"That sounds like it could take all night," said Torie. "Hey, want me to try another spell to make them combine the way we want?"

"No, no," said Jasmin quickly. "Do that wrong and it could blow this house sky high. Even I wouldn't try to cast a spell like that." She huffed and put her hands on her sides. "Looks like I'll have to do this the old-fashioned way and hope I stumble onto the right batch sooner rather than later."

"I can help with that," said Elric. He had been standing in the doorway watching them.

"How can you help?" said Jasmin. She hadn't meant for the words to come out as sharply as they did.

"Well, I can smell all of that from here. When we were in Trinity and I chased the killer, it smelled like all of the stuff you have on the table."

Both Torie and Jasmin stared at him, eyebrows raised, as if to say "and?"

"Wolves have the best sense of smell of any supernatural. I can sniff out what, and how much of those for you to put together and recreate whatever the magic was that masked the killer."

As one, their eyes widened in understanding.

"Elric, my man," said Jasmin. "Have I ever told you that you are my new best friend? Step right on up, honey."

## 23

As it turned out, it wasn't as easy as Elric had suggested. Granted, he could make out all of the ingredients, but knowing exactly the ratio was a little harder than he thought it would be. Stepping back, he regarded the powders and herbs and knew there was only one way to make it work.

"I need to shift," he said. "In my wolf form, I can sift through the layers, determine the exact makeup of each."

"But then you can't tell me how much of what to use," said Jasmin.

"No; but he can tell me," said Torie.

Jasmin looked at her friend, realizing there was no other option. Nodding, she watched as Elric dropped into his wolf form and then leapt gracefully up onto the table.

"Well I never," said Alva's ghost. "Allowing a wolf to put its paws on my table like that."

Torie ignored her, reaching out to touch Elric's mind instead.

Elric sniffed carefully at the first jar of silver powder, letting the scent run through his nose to his brain.

"He says add a little of this stuff until he says stop," Torie said.

Jasmin did as she was told, using a baking spoon to carefully scoop a small amount at a time into a large mortar.

"That's enough!" said Torie as Elric moved to another of the open jars, taking a delicate sniff and closing his eyes.

"He says there was more of this; twice as much as the silver powder."

After moving on and repeating instructions, he would go back to the mortar and smell the mixture again, making sure it was becoming what he remembered. When he got to the first of the dried herbs he sniffed and then paused.

"He says this is one of the properties in the mixture, but that it smelled different. He said this one smells like the earth, but what the killer wore was a more liquid form of the same thing," said Torie.

"A liquid form?" asked Jasmin. "Does he mean it was boiled and then added?"

Torie closed her eyes and listened. She shook her head. "No, he said it was wetter...but he's not sure how."

"That's nightshade," said Alva, drifting nearer the table. "It can't be boiled, but you can grind it down into a paste."

"Yes!" Torie relayed. "He thinks that's what it was."

Without taking her eyes off the table, Jasmin held out her hand and a large, marble pestle flew to her. She used it to start grinding out the nightshade.

"Hey, can you teach me to do that?" said Torie. "It would really come in handy."

"There's nothing to it. When you're starting out and magic is new to you, you just look at the object you want, and then call to it... imagine it in your hand. It's one of the easier summoning spells."

Torie looked around and saw a small tin cup on a shelf on the far wall. Holding out her hand, she pictured the cup sitting in her palm.

Nothing.

She cleared her throat and loudly said, "Cup, come to my hand."

Nothing.

Jasmin stopped grinding and looked up at her. "I didn't mean to literally call to it. It's an inanimate object after all, not a dog." She looked up at Elric and shrugged. "Sorry, no offense."

Torie ignored her friend's banter. Maybe the cup was too big? Should she start with something smaller?

There was a silver thimble on the shelf as well. Surely there wasn't much that was more light-weight than that. Again, she held out her hand and concentrated. She saw the thimble flying through space and landing in her hand, just as Jasmin had so casually done. She had also seen her mother do it, so in her mind there was no reason she couldn't do it as well.

Again, nothing. The thimble didn't even so much as wiggle.

She looked back at Jasmin, realizing the other woman was speaking to her.

"I'm sorry, what was that?"

"I said, how is this?" Jasmine had ground the nightshade down into a sticky paste.

Torie glanced in Elric's direction and nodded. "He says that's the right consistency. Half the amount you have showing."

Before long, Elric looked at Torie and nodded his head before leaping off the table and shifting to human in mid-air. He landed with his backside to the women, his hands covering his private parts as he made for the back of the house with his clothes in tow.

"Not that I'm complaining about the view," said Jasmin, "but we really need to teach him how to shift and keep his clothes. It's basic shifter magic and he needs to learn it."

Torie didn't say anything, and that didn't go unnoticed by Jasmin.

"Unless you like seeing him all flapping in the breeze like that?"

Torie blushed and quickly changed the subject. "So that's the potion, huh? Do you know what it is?" She looked at the amber-colored liquid in the mortar, leaning in to sniff it as if it were cake batter waiting to be poured.

"Don't get too close, and don't breathe it in," warned Jasmin, waving her off. "Yes, I know exactly what this is, and I also have a good idea who we are dealing with as well."

"So...are you going to tell me?" Torie's heart was racing, and she could feel her palms growing sweaty with excitement.

"It's a variation of a sleep potion. Well, to be more accurate, it's a cross between a sleep spell and a forget-me-now potion."

"Forget-me-now? What is that?"

"It's an old-world potion created by thieves back in ancient Persia. It was designed to be blown into the face of anyone that captured the bearer of the potion. It was so potent that it was capable of causing the recipient to instantly forget what they were just doing; or who was just standing in front of them."

"That would explain why Eddie and my mother have blank spots in their memory."

Jasmin nodded. "But here's the thing. It doesn't work on paranormal beings. That's where the addition of the sleep potion additive came into play. That would boost it to work on supernaturals. It would send them into a deep comatose state, leaving them defenseless against the killer."

"But why add the amnesia part to the mix if the sleep spell was all they needed?"

"I'm not sure. It could be that one part of the potion alone may not have been enough. Or it could have been a back-up."

Torie's eyes lit up. "In case the victim ever got away, like Eddie. It would ensure they couldn't identify the killer."

"Bingo," answered Jasmin.

"So we know how it was done," said Torie, "and you said you have an idea as to who or what we are dealing with?"

Jasmin's eyes narrowed. "Yes. This is definitely the work of a witch, but not our kind. This was created by a hedge witch. They specialize in perverting nature's gifts into dark potions. They are also dabblers in the kind of magic they can steal or mimic from others."

"What do you mean?"

"Well, you and I, and all of our true sisters, are born with magic. It just doesn't get unlocked until later in life for us. But we have a natural connection with the energies around us; we can manipulate it to do our bidding. Hedges are different. They aren't born with power and it doesn't reside within them. They learn it; cobble it together bit by bit. They work with roots and are very adept at creating potions. Low level magics can usually be performed by them, but they are miles away from being in our class."

"So one of these hedges is going around killing shifters? For what?"

"Hedges are typically loners. They don't even congregate in groups with one another for fear that some other hedge will steal what they have or copy what they know. They are a nuisance and generally looked down upon, but I've never heard of one being dangerous. And they certainly wouldn't try attacking a shifter; that's way out of their league."

They were both quiet, contemplating what they had just learned.

"What about the blood sample Max gave you?" said Torie.

Jasmin walked over to her purse and retrieved the sample, sitting it on the table between them.

"We can use this to trace the person it came from. But we have to be careful with the spell we cast. Blood magic is serious business."

"But it can lead us to the hedge witch. Maybe we don't have to wait for them to attack us. We can go on the offense."

Jasmin nodded slowly. "Maybe. Or maybe this isn't from a hedge."

Torie looked at her questioningly. "But Max caught them killing Taylor. It has to be the same one that broke into the vet's office in Trinity."

"Exactly. But judging from their description of what happened, I'm not so sure that was the hedge. They aren't supernatural creatures. They certainly can't outrun or fight off a werewolf. Something isn't right here," Jasmin said, rubbing her temples in frustration.

"Aspirin?" offered Torie.

"That would be great."

Rather than go and get it from the medicine cabinet in the bathroom, Torie held out her hand and again firmly said, "Aspirin."

Again, nothing happened. She frowned and shook her head as she made her way to the bathroom.

"Give it time," called Jasmin after her as she went back to

studying the vial of blood and the mixture in front of her. By the time Torie returned with two white tablets and a cup of water, she had an idea.

"Maybe, we can still make this work," she said. "We can cast a tracking spell on the blood, and also use it to mix in with this nasty little potion the hedge witch cooked up. That would make the owner of the blood even more susceptible to the sleep spell than anyone he or she would have used it on."

Torie thought for a moment, her brow furrowed. "What if it doesn't work? Do we fight? What kind of a chance do we really stand against something that can defeat a werewolf?" She was trying not to panic at the thought. "Maybe we should let the cops handle it."

Jasmin put her hands on her hips. "What do you mean what kind of chance do we stand? Two badass witches and a couple of shifters? We are nobody's joke."

"I hardly qualify. I can't even summon objects, and um, Fionna is a squirrel."

"Yeah, with really sharp teeth."

They both burst out laughing at that. It was nice to know they hadn't lost their sense of humor; even on the possible eve of their deaths.

"Alright. Time to get serious," said Jasmin.

She removed the cap from the vial and carefully added two drops of blood into the potion. Instantly, the contents of the mortar began to smoke and hiss.

"Is that normal?" questioned Torie.

Jasmin shrugged. "No idea. Obviously what we are dealing with isn't entirely human, so who knows. Alva? You seen this before?"

Alva shimmered next to them. "You must have done something wrong," she said. "That only happens if you add the blood of something dead."

She leaned over the brew and whispered something in a language Torie didn't understand. The brew settled down, turning murky and then crimson at Jasmin's words.

"You have got to teach me that as well. What language was that?"

"A language older than any that is still spoken in this world. You will be surprised at how quickly you'll pick it up. It is the language of hexes, and once you are exposed to it, you will become fluent in no time."

Torie nodded, looking at the putrid liquid. "What do we do now?"

"Get me a small empty jar to put it in. Then, we activate the tracking spell and go find this bastard."

Torie looked at the jar on a shelf and started to try summoning it. The thought of failure was too much for her to handle and, with a sigh, she walked over and grabbed it, passing it to Jasmin who gingerly began filling it with the potion.

"Now, go get Elric and Fionna. It's time."

When she returned with their friends at her side, Jasmin placed the vial with the remaining blood on the floor in front of her.

"Take my hands, Torie," she said, reaching out. They clasped hands above the vial. "Repeat after me, and envision the spell finding the killer."

*"Oh daughter of the moon, of wax and wane,*
*send this blood back, from whence it came!"*

Torie closed her eyes and began reciting the spell with Jasmin. Together, they repeated the incantation four times before Jasmin stopped and dropped Torie's hands.

The vial of blood ruptured, sending dark red tendrils of smoke into the air. It roiled, gathering into an angry cloud that looked like a thunderhead with the dying light of a sunset shining through. Rising, it swirled between them and then headed for the windows at the front of the house.

"Follow it!" said Jasmin. "It should take us right to the—"

Before she could finish her sentence, the cloud stopped, spinning in place like a small dust devil, before splitting open in a shower of crimson sparks and disappearing.

"What happened?" asked Torie. "Did the spell not work?"

"No, it worked," said Jasmin. "I can't imagine why it would just stop like that. Unless..."

Just then, Torie's mother shimmered, her form becoming dimmer, her face a mask of surprise and fear.

"Torie! Run...there is something wicked heading this way!"

But before anyone could respond, the front door shattered inward under the force of a powerful kick. A figure dressed in black, face covered in the darkness of a black hood, stepped inside.

"Forgive me, witches," it said in a raspy voice. "I am commanded to kill all of you; but first you will turn over whatever evidence you have. Do that, and I will make your deaths painless."

And then, faster than any of the women could react, it launched itself at them.

## 24

Torie was the closest to the shadow, and she felt a sudden burning on the side of her face as it struck her before racing on towards Jasmin.

It was close to making contact, when a large blur broadsided it. Elric, in full wolf form, knocked the killer sideways into the wall, pouncing on the creature with a roar that nearly deafened all in the room. Despite his size and the ferocity of his attack, the shadow figure had regained its balance. It struck out with a fist, and Elric howled in pain.

Fionna leapt to his side, taking up an iron poker from the fireplace and bringing it down with all her strength onto the creature's head. She heard a satisfying grunt of pain before an open-handed slap sent her spiraling across the room.

Jasmin whirred into action; reaching into her purse, she pulled out the jar that contained the potion she and Torie had created. She raised her hand to throw it at the shadow, only to suddenly find her arm locked in mid-air, enclosed in a grip of iron. The killer had become a blur, rushing to her before she could even throw it. She screamed in pain as the grip on her forearm tightened and she knew that at any moment the bones in her arm would shatter.

"No!" screamed Torie, throwing her hands out. Again, the same force she had felt at the vet's office flew out of her, sending the killer and Jasmin tumbling across the room to crash into the kitchen.

Before either of them could react, Elric was in his hybrid werewolf form and sprinting to their side. He grabbed the killer from behind, locking his powerful arms around him. Fionna ran to his side, throwing herself around the attacker's legs, adding her own shifter strength to Elric's to hold him fast.

It was at that moment Torie moved to pick up the jar Jasmin had dropped. She loosened the cap just as Elric and Fionna were losing their hold on the more powerful killer.

"Go to sleep!" she said, throwing the contents into the shadow's face.

Immediately, the figure slumped, held aloft in Elric's arms.

"It's not completely out," said Elric, his voice sounded like rocks being churned in a cement mixture. "It's fighting the spell!"

Jasmin was on her feet and moved to stand in front of them. She reached up and snatched back the hood revealing the killer's face. Her hand flew to her mouth in horror.

"Arnold?" she said. "It can't be."

But it was. The vampire's head lolled, his chin on his chest. The potion should have put him to sleep, but he resisted, lifting his face to Jasmin's. His eyes were red, his lips drawn back in a grimace.

"Jasmin," he said weakly, "please...I don't want to hurt anyone. I can't stop myself...you need to get out of here before..." his voice trailed off and his head dropped.

"Before what?" she urged, backing up to stand next to Torie.

Still held fast in Elric's grasp, Arnold snapped to attention, his face a mask of hatred and anger as he looked at Jasmin.

"Before I have to hurt you all."

He roared in defiance, raising his arms to break free of Elric's hold. He lashed out again, sending both Torie and Jasmin sprawling. Then, pivoting on one leg, he cast off Fionna and turned to face Elric.

Twisting free of the werewolf, he snapped one of Elric's arms, relishing in the yelp of pain it elicited. Then, using his superior strength, he grabbed the wolf, one arm around his waist, and with the other he grabbed Elric's shock of hair, pulling his head back so that the werewolf's throat was exposed. He leaned back, extending his fangs to their full length, and leaned in, targeting the lycanthrope's neck.

Torie was on her knees, watching the horror unfold. There was nothing she could do. Her head hurt from multiple blows, and her lungs screamed for oxygen. She watched helplessly as the creature that had killed her mother, and was about to kill someone she was just beginning to develop feelings for, lowered his teeth, his weapons, onto Elric's throat.

No.

This was not something she would allow. No one else was going to die under her watch. She felt a swelling of strength she had never known as her magic bubbled up inside of her, waiting for her call. She held out her hand.

"Fangs!" she said, her voice powerful and resolute.

Instantly, her hand was filled with what felt like hard, slick rocks. She looked down and realized they weren't rocks at all; but rather, shiny white, very pointy, teeth covered in red saliva.

She dropped them in disgust as she looked up at Arnold.

The now de-fanged vampire stood in shock, one hand covering his mouth, blood seeping through his fingers. He had dropped Elric, and the werewolf was struggling to get enough oxygen into his system to quench the fire that threatened to burn through his lungs.

Fionna crept up slowly behind them, her hand at her side, holding something that Torie couldn't make out.

No, not holding...covered in something. There was a glint of light as it reflected off the object over her fist. Arnold sensed her presence at the last minute and turned. But it was too late. She sent her fist rocketing into his jaw. The vampire's head snapped around and he dropped like a puppet with cut strings.

Torie ran over to them, looking from the collapsed vampire to Fionna, who was shaking her hand and grimacing in pain.

"What is that?" asked Torie incredulously as she pointed to Fionna's hand.

"Solid silver brass knuckles," Fionna said. "Sometimes, old-school is the best school."

"Where did you get something like that?"

"From me," said Elric, now fully human and massaging a bruised shoulder. "Living in a place like this, with a potentially supernatural killer running around targeting shifters, you can't be too careful." He winked at Fionna, giving her a warm smile.

Jasmin stumbled up to them, one hand on her head as she surveyed the fallen vampire.

"Jasmin, are you okay?" asked Torie, examining her friend's forehead.

"Nothing that a couple weeks of sleep and a few bottles of Midol won't fix," she said.

Bending down, she checked Arnold, placing a finger on his neck.

"Is he...alive?" asked Fionna.

"I have no idea," Jasmin said. "Vampires don't have a pulse, so I guess. I mean, he didn't turn into ash or a puff of smoke, so that must be a good thing, right?"

"Do they do that?" questioned Torie.

"No. They don't," said Elric. "They are notoriously hard to kill. You have to remove their head and then burn it." He bent down, reaching for the unconscious vampire.

"No!" said Torie. "I mean, don't do it; at least not here. It sounds like it would be really gross."

"Um, you just ripped all his teeth out," said Elric.

Torie blushed. "But, I mean, it sounded like he didn't know what he was doing. Or at least he wasn't in control."

"She's right," said Jasmin. "He kept telling us to run; that he couldn't stop himself. I think he was just a tool that someone was using."

"You think the hedge witch is behind all of this?" said Torie.

Jasmin nodded. "Who else would be stupid enough to create a

potion that could bring a vampire under their thrall? Especially one as old as Arnold. The question is why would one attempt this?"

"What do we do with him?" asked Fionna. "I don't know much about vampire physiology, but I'm betting he won't be out for long."

Torie looked at Elric. "I don't suppose you have silver chains, do you?"

Elric's eyes grew wide. "Actually, I do! But by the time I get them and get back—"

"He could be awake and ready for round two," finished Jasmin.

"He killed Taylor. I say we let Elric finish him," said Fionna.

"Works for me," came a voice from behind them. A diminutive figure stepped into the room through the broken doorway. "Saves me the trouble of having to do it myself."

"Breonna?" said Jasmin. "Are you—?"

"Yep," said the vampire's assistant. "I'm all hedged out."

She pulled a vial from the pocket of the jacket she wore and threw it to the ground. It shattered on impact, releasing a thick smoke that split into two clouds, each billowing towards the two shifters. Both Fionna and Elric dropped to the ground when it assaulted them, flooding their systems with sleeping potion.

Jasmin quickly raised a hand, swirling it in mid-air, creating a gust of wind that was strong enough to carry the magical smoke out the door and away from herself and Torie.

"Nice," said Breonna. "I'm not here for you two. I just need one more shifter and then I swear I'll be out of this town for good. You'll never have to see me again."

Torie took a step to the side, putting some distance between her and Jasmin without taking her eyes off the young hedge witch.

"Is that why you've been having Arnold hunt them? Harvest blood and whatever else from them? What are you doing with shifters?" Torie asked.

Breonna shrugged. Her affect was flat and emotionless. "I'm not doing anything with them. I'm just doing what I was paid to do. What they do with the shifter parts they ask for...not my business."

Before Torie could ask who *they* were, the hedge witch reached into another pocket, taking out a second vial. She drew her arm back to throw it at the witches. But this time Torie was faster. She threw her hands out, blasting Breonna away from them and sending the vial clattering out the door.

Jasmin approached Breonna before she could make her way to her feet. She held out both hands and said:

*"Unclean creature I bind you in place,*
*locking you now in time and space."*

The spell wrapped around Breonna like quicksand, freezing her where she lay. The girl's eyes looked around frantically as she realized she couldn't move. Her face twisted wildly as her anger began to turn to fear. "What...what did you do to me?" she mouthed, her words slurred by her inability to properly control her lips and tongue.

"Just a little spell that will keep you nice and still for us while you tell us what's going on," said Jasmin.

Breonna's frozen eyes hardened. "I'm not telling you anything. Because I don't know anything."

"We'll see about that," said Jasmin. Elric was beginning to stir, and she made her way over to help him to his feet.

He saw the hedge witch locked in place and a growl escaped his throat as he walked over to her.

"Do you recognize her scent?" asked Jasmin.

Elric nodded his head. "Yes, she is the source of the magic that cloaks the vampire."

"You don't scare me," said Breonna. "You old witches don't have the balls to take out Arnold; and he killed a lot of your friends. Stop posturing and let me go. Maybe we can work something out."

Something in her tone, her smugness, her youthful cockiness, struck at Torie. She walked over to the young witch and pulled her hair back until she was looking up at them.

"Little girl, let me tell you something," said Jasmin. "This is not Buffy and you are most definitely not the chosen one. I will not think twice about letting this wolf eat you."

"Wait," said Torie, her voice cold and calm, "I have a better idea." She leaned over Breonna and smiled. "You saw what I did to Arnold. I wonder what I can pull out of you?"

She held her hand out, palm up, in front of the wide-eyed girl.

"What is it that a hedge witch would be most afraid of losing? Oh, I know..." she narrowed her gaze and stared at the girl before speaking a single word. "Fingers—"

"No!" screamed Breonna, stopping the summoning. "I don't know much but I'll tell you what I can. Just don't finish that; please."

Jasmin looked at Torie and nodded.

"Okay, then talk," said Torie.

"I've never met the man before; the guy that hired me. He just gave me a list of very specific parts, organs, bones, that he needed from shifters."

"What was he doing with them?" asked Jasmin.

"I don't know. He just said he wanted to—" Her voice trailed off and her eyes grew wide.

"What?" said Torie. "He wanted to do what?"

But this time when Breonna answered it was not the same voice they had just spoken to. It was deep and raspy; one that reminded Torie of that little girl from *The Exorcist.*

"No, little witches. You will not learn anything from this one. But soon, maybe sooner than you know, we'll have a chat in person."

With that, Breonna's eyes rolled back in her head and her face went slack. A foul-smelling vapor escaped her open mouth. She moaned, deep in the back of her throat before her head slumped forward and she breathed her last breath.

Torie jumped back, both hands over her mouth to stifle a scream.

Jasmin waved her hand, releasing the body from the spell that held it in place.

"Jesus," she said. "I've never seen anything like that before." She walked over and placed two fingers on Breonna's neck. "Wow. Dead as a doornail."

"What now?" said Fionna.

"Now we call the sheriff," said Torie. "And give him the body of a killer."

There was a muffled moan and they turned to see Arnold sitting up. He looked around the room before reaching a hand tenderly to his mouth.

"What happened...is she dead?" he said, his words muffled and wet.

"You're okay," said Jasmin. She went over to her friend and helped him to his feet. "Do you remember what happened?"

Arnold's face grew slack, his eyes began to dart back and forth wildly. "Oh no. What have I done? All those shifters...I...oh no, Taylor!"

Jasmin caught him as he collapsed forward.

"I am so, so sorry. I didn't have control. I didn't want to do any of those things. I wanted to stop. I even tried to kill myself once, but I couldn't do it." He looked around the room at everyone. "You should kill me now. I don't want to ever be in that situation again."

"She's gone," said Torie. "I am betting with her death, the spell that controlled you is broken as well."

Torie's mother appeared in a wisp of smoke that took on her transparent form.

"She's right," said Alva. "I have my memories back. I remember what happened that day I was... I was killed. She was with you. She threw some type of dust on you and whispered in your ear. Then you attacked me and Ellie. But it wasn't your fault, Arnold." She choked back tears, but for Arnold it was all too much. His eyes welled up and red tears flowed down his cheeks.

In the distance, sirens whined. Seconds later the inside of the house was illuminated by flashing red and blue strobe lights as the sheriff and his deputies surveyed and secured the scene.

"So, you're telling me that all of this—" he looked around at the destroyed living area— "was done by that little girl right there?" He glanced at the body that lay crumpled on the floor.

"Yes,' said Torie. "She showed up, crazed out of her mind...probably drunk off one of her own potions, and demanded we turn over whatever evidence we had that could have implicated her in the killings of the shifters. She was pretty spry for a hedge witch." She hesitated before continuing. "Also, we're pretty sure she wasn't acting alone. Someone, or something, else was calling the shots."

The sheriff huffed, giving her a side-eyed look as he walked around the space. He wrinkled his nose and sniffed the air. Torie stiffened, but Jasmin reached out and took her hand. The sheriff was a supernatural, but he didn't have the physical senses of a shifter, and as far as Jasmin knew, none of his deputies were shifters.

"What is that smell?" he said, looking around.

Torie tensed up, but Jasmine stepped forward and spoke reassuringly to him. "That's whatever nasty little potion she brewed to take out the shifters before she carved them up. No idea why she did that, but if I were you, I wouldn't try breathing in too much of that. No idea what it would do to a dwarf."

Instantly the sheriff put a hand to his mouth and stepped back.

"Mother Nature, I've about had enough of this crazy town," he whispered. He sighed, speaking up to the two women. "So I'll need you to come by the station and make a formal statement."

"And you'll let Max go?" asked Torie.

"Yes. He's locked up tight so no way he had anything to do with this. It just seems like we are missing something. But if you're convinced this is the killer, then I'm happy to declare this case closed."

"This is definitely our killer," Torie said. "Who knows why killers do the things they do. Especially in this case."

He nodded and headed back to supervise the loading of the body into the M.E's van.

"Thank you," Torie said to Jasmin.

"No, thank you. We couldn't have done this without you. Welcome to the club. You're going to be one powerful witch." She hesitated, looking at her friend. "So, were you really going to take her fingers?"

Torie smiled. "Absolutely. She'd have mixed her last batch of poison, that's for sure."

They both laughed and watched as the sheriff and his team left. Once they were gone, Elric and Fionna came out of the back room, and Alva shimmered into view.

Fionna had her arm around Arnold.

"You should have let them take me," said Arnold.

"Nonsense," replied Torie. "The real killer is still out there. We may have foiled him or her for now...but I'm willing to bet we haven't heard the last of them. You've suffered enough at their hands. We all have." She looked at Fionna. "I think it's time this community began to heal again."

She reached over and gave his arm a squeeze.

## 25

The inside of Jim's Best was bustling. The heaviness of the past couple of weeks had finally evaporated and the bakery was filled with the sounds of laughter and the smell of freshly baked goods and gourmet coffee.

The ladies sat in their usual chairs, a small plate of assorted mini-scones and two French presses sat on the coffee table in front of them.

"It finally feels right in here again," said Fionna, reaching for one of the tiny blueberry scones. "Well, almost."

No one needed to ask what she meant. They all missed Taylor and the carefree light and attitude she always brought with her wherever she went.

"So, Elric," said Jasmin, "how's Max settling in to his new position?"

Elric sat next to Torie, sipping on a cup of coffee.

"He's doing surprisingly well," he said. "I think being a sheriff is his calling."

They weren't surprised. Dwayne had turned in his badge shortly after wrapping up the case. As it turned out, he wasn't cut out for the type of work that involved shifter killers and angry witches. He had returned to his previous life in the woods where he was happy, and his skill with stonework was already in demand by the townspeople. The women had seen him a couple of times since he retired. He would drive around town hauling lumber or rock to various sites and home restoration projects. He'd nod and wave; always with a smile on his face.

"Yeah, Dwayne never seemed cut out for that job," said Jasmin. "I'm just surprised that none of his deputies wanted the position."

"Oh, I'm sure they did," said Fionna. "But none of them were ready to stand up to an alpha wolf to take it."

"Speaking of alphas," said Torie, turning to Elric.

He blushed. "Max released me. He has a whole new pack now. Granted, they're human and don't quite understand why they can't say no to him, but he saw that the two of us are in different, and better, places now."

Torie smiled. That made her happy. She hadn't been looking forward to trying to devise a spell that would break a bond between an alpha and beta. She looked at the wolf sitting next to her and felt a wave of happiness that she hadn't expected to ever find again at this point in her life. It was still new of course. They were taking baby steps—no, that wasn't right. What came before baby steps? Crawling? Yes, that was what they were doing; they were baby crawling together.

She was learning what it was like to have a man that wanted to listen to her, no matter what she wanted to talk about. It was nice. But she didn't feel the need to rush anything this time. This was her second act, and so far, it was blowing act one to smithereens. He sensed her watching him and looked up, smiling and giving her a slight nod. Impulsively, she reached over and took his hand.

Jasmin noticed and gave them both a smile. Not that Torie needed affirmation, but it was nice knowing that her fledging relationship, although she was loath to give it a name, had been blessed.

She watched the new friends she had made; warmth spreading through her making her feel positively radiant. How had she been so lucky? At a time when she thought, or rather *knew*, she had lost everything, was when she came alive. She felt like she had spent forty years sleep-walking and someone had just thrown a bucket of cold water on her. Every part of her being was alive and tingling with possibility.

She thought about the new friends she had made, some she had already lost in such a short time, and her resolve to make this place and its community her new home. She felt the sting of tears threaten to run down her face as she realized just how much she loved Singing Falls.

Not that it was perfect of course; no place was. But it was close enough.

"What about your mother?" said Fionna. "I don't know anything about ghosts. Is it like in the movies; when their murder is solved they fade away and go into the afterlife?"

"It hasn't happened like that yet," said Torie. "She's still around, coming and going when I need to talk to her...or sometimes when she needs to talk to me. She can't leave the house though, so I suppose there is something to being tethered to the place you passed in. But it's good. We're in a good place, as strange as that sounds."

"Doesn't sound strange at all," said Jasmin. "Strange lives in this town, and you're a part of that now."

"Speaking of strange," said Fionna, "has anyone checked on Eddie lately?"

The shifter had finally healed completely and had resumed working in the towns artisanal pizza shop. Torie had to admit that he made a mean fig and prosciutto pizza.

"He's been hanging around with Arnold lately," said Jasmin quietly. At the mention of the vampire's name, Fionna tensed up, and Torie reached over to place a comforting hand on her knee.

"I'm not so certain there isn't something brewing between the two of them," continued Jasmin. "Of course, they have issues to work out as well, but they're trying."

Torie nodded. Once he was healed, Eddie told them that he remembered going over to Arnold's house the night he was attacked. The two had just started to date and were trying to keep everything quiet. He said that Arnold hadn't seemed himself that night and at one point had told Eddie that he really needed to leave. Eddie assumed he was having second thoughts about their budding relationship, but then, in the snap of a finger, Arnold had changed.

He attacked Eddie, and the shifter knew he was trying to kill him. He had escaped, but only just, shifting and fleeing just as Arnold had thrown some kind of powder at him that made him dizzy. Because he was shifting at the same time, he didn't get the full dose of the potion, but it was still enough to slow him down, until he eventually collapsed. He tried shifting back to his human form, and that helped him stumble far enough that he could make it to the road. That was where Torie had met him.

Thinking back on it, she realized that Eddie had probably given them a clue as to who their assailant was when the wolves had found him unconscious the morning her mother was killed. They had found him passed out on a cleared ledge; in the only area of open sunlight. He had sought to escape Arnold yet again and took refuge in the one place the vampire couldn't reach him.

"So, how is Arnold doing with the whole, you know...?" asked Torie, motioning to her mouth.

"He's coping," said Jasmin. "Vampires are like sharks; they lose a tooth and another grows back in its place. It's slow, and painful, but it's also a reminder of what he became. It's his way of paying penance."

"Torie, what are your plans now?" asked Fionna. "You're definitely staying in town?"

She smiled. "Yes. My mother was right. There is something about this town, quirks and all, that calls to me."

She was ready to put her old life to rest. Everything she owned back in New York had been sold to pay into a fund meant for the families that had been harmed by her ex-husband's predatory business. As luck would have it, the money her mother had left her could not be touched, and it was more than enough for her to continue paying for Shawn's education. She could easily afford to buy a new house in town but had chosen to invest in renovations on her mother's house; much to ghost Alva's dismay.

"Oh, how's the book coming?" asked Jasmin.

Torie groaned. "Slow. But I'm getting there."

As part of her path along the hexing arts, Jasmin had suggested that Torie create her own grimoire. A book of custom spells and potions she was creating. It was taxing and amusing at the same time. But she was excited to learn to harness her magic in ways she had never thought possible. Her natural telepathic abilities with shifters was still her strongest ability, but with Jasmin and Alva's help, she was learning.

"Well, I don't know about you all, but I am looking forward to some down time," said Fionna. "It will be nice to enjoy Singing Falls in peace and quiet for a while."

The chime of a bell rang through the space as the front door to the bakery opened.

A woman, wearing a long white dress with intricate embroidery, flowed into the room. Her hair was nearly as white as her dress and dotted with small gemstones and flower petals. Part of Torie's learning had been recognizing the various supernaturals that lived in and about Singing Falls. This lady was a faerie, through and through. She looked around, barely able to contain her anxiety. Finally, her eyes settled on them.

She hurried over and gave them a rather clumsy half-bow.

"Forgive me," she said, her voice sounding almost musical to their ears, "but are you the ladies that recently dealt with—" she looked around and then lowered her voice, "the situation with the individual that was harming the shifters?"

Torie stood and approached her. "Yes, that would be us. Are you okay? You look nervous."

"Forgive my intrusion," the fae said, "but I was wondering if you might help me." She fished around in a small, blue bag that she carried with her and removed a photo. "This is my daughter. She disappeared a couple of months ago. We spoke almost every day and then, out of the blue, she stopped calling me. No text, no letter, no emails. It is like she just disappeared from the face of the earth. We share a connection, she and I...and try as I might, I can no longer 'feel' her." The woman stopped, steadying herself before she could continue. "The last I heard she was working at starting her own business far away from Singing Falls. She always said this town was too sleepy for her. She had also started to date someone, but she wouldn't tell me who. Then she broke off contact, and never came back home. I told her many times the world of man is no place for one such as she, but she was obsessed with it. Can you help me find her? I can pay you whatever you want."

Torie smiled, trying to comfort the distraught woman. She took the photograph from her and felt the blood drain from her face when she looked at the picture.

"Torie," said Fionna. "What is it? Are you okay?"

Torie dropped into the seat, her eyes focused on something far away as she handed the photograph over to Fionna.

"The woman in this picture," she whispered, "her name is Wednesday; she's the business partner my husband left me for."

No one said a word. Torie felt the indescribable pain of old wounds tearing open. She looked at Fionna. Life in Singing Falls was about to become anything but peaceful and quiet.

BOOK TWO IS AVAILABLE AT: That Good Hex

THE END

If you enjoyed this book, feel free to try these other works by M.J. Caan, including the complete Trinity Cove trilogy, and sign up for MJ's mailing list for news about book 2 in this ongoing series: https://sendfox.com/MJauthor

**Trinity Cove Shifter Wars Trilogy**
The Girl With The Good Magic: The Shifter Wars Book One
Enter The Wolf: The Shifter Wars Book Two
The Return Of The Witch

# ALSO BY M.J. CAAN

The Trinity Cove Trilogy

The Girl With The Good Magic: The Shifter Wars Book One

Enter The Wolf: The Shifter Wars Book Two

The Return Of The Witch

RH Gargoyle Series

Bound

# ABOUT THE AUTHOR

M.J. Caan is a science fiction and fantasy author living in North Carolina. When not convening with the spirit world via keyboard to create fantastical new worlds, M.J. can be found cuddling with a very energetic Australian Shepherd that is too spoiled for her own good.

If you like this book, please leave a review. If you would like to contact M.J. please don't hesitate to reach out via email or Facebook. I can always be reached at:

mjcaan@gmail.com